TROUBLE
RIDER

Also published in Large Print
from G.K. Hall by Thomas Thompson:

King of Abilene
Bitter Water
Outlaw Valley
Shadow of the Butte

Thomas Thompson

TROUBLE
RIDER

G·K·Hall&C?
Boston, Massachusetts
1993

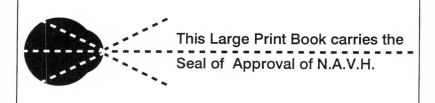

This Large Print Book carries the Seal of Approval of N.A.V.H.

First Printed 1956.

Published in Large Print by arrangement with Thomas Thompson, in care of the Brandt and Brandt Literary Agents, Inc.

G.K. Hall Large Print Book Series.

Printed on acid free paper in the United States of America.

Set in 16 pt. Plantin.

Library of Congress Cataloging-in-Publication Data

Thompson, Thomas, 1913–
    Trouble rider / Thomas Thompson.
        p.   cm.—(G.K. Hall large print book series)
    (Nightingale series)
      ISBN 0-8161-5480-5 (acid-free paper)
      1. Large type books. I. title
    [PS3539.H697T76   1993]
    813′.54—dc20

92-41193

FOR
JUDY,
WHO IS EVERYTHING I WANTED
IN A DAUGHTER

CHAPTER
1

As HE RODE up the slope toward the town's only livery stable he could hear the muttering river sounds above the pelt of the Oregon rain. His thoughts matched the mood of the weather, but his fist-bruised face didn't show it. He reined up in front of the stable, folded his big, ungloved hands on the saddle horn and immediately relaxed, a man who had learned to take his rest when and where he found it. Behind him the sky was low, a tumbling grey mass saturated with water, and the greyness lay over the sage and juniper slopes and dulled the first show of spring grass on the valley floor. For a moment he was part of the sombre, threatening landscape, a man who was looking for the best while expecting the worst, like winter seeking summer through a turbulent spring. He grinned and the impression was lost. The stableman glanced up at the rider and made his old joke. "Do you think you'll ever

1

amount to much, Hardisty?" the stableman said.

"Hadn't you heard?" Wayne Hardisty said. "I'm gonna stock the state of Montana with Oregon cattle." He swung down as easily as if he had slept last night. "Take good care of my horse, Pete."

The stableman looked at Hardisty and tried to avoid seeing the split lip and the fist-marked face. He said, "With the credit you've got I ought to feed him bedding straw and tie him in the rain."

"But you won't, Pete," Wayne Hardisty said. "I'm gonna be a big man around here. I'll remember my friends."

"At the rate you're going, the only friend you're gonna have left is the undertaker," Pete said. "I'm expecting him to come up here any day and ask me for your measurements." The stableman expelled his breath as if he had been holding it too long and his shoulders drooped and the bantering pretence was gone. He was suddenly an old friend with an old friend's worry. "I don't know what it was about, Wayne," he said, "but it ought never to have happened. A thing like that's no good, Wayne."

"News gets around," Wayne Hardisty said.

"When two brothers get into a fist fight and half kill each other, it does," Pete said. "Now tell me it's none of my business."

"I don't have to tell you," Wayne said. "You already know it."

"Does Ruth know about it?"

A small anger touched Wayne and found its way into his voice. "An old family friend gets away with asking a hell of a lot of questions, don't he, Pete?"

"I don't like to see brothers fighting over a woman," Pete said doggedly.

"Is that what it was?"

"Sorry," Pete said. "I had to have my say."

"All right. You've had it," Wayne said. He tilted his head toward the stable door. "Are they here yet?"

"They're here," Pete said. "They've been here a half-hour. From the looks of 'em I'd say you could give Montana back to the Indians and push Oregon into the Columbia River." The stableman cocked an eye at the little town that lay at the foot of the slope. He seemed to be looking back into time. "Do you really expect to deliver a herd of a thousand cows, Wayne?"

A grin touched Wayne Hardisty's eyes. "I expect to," he said. "I signed a contract with a man back in Montana telling him I would."

"Was that contract for cows that hadn't eaten for two months?" Pete asked.

"Nope," Wayne said. "Fat cows. And that's what the man will get.

He pushed by Pete and entered the stable. It was warm and dry, and thick with the smell of hay and horses and leather. Two men were sitting on an overturned packing case, their backs to each other. One was whittling; the other was staring at his folded hands. Wayne greeted them briefly. "Bob, Lee." He stood there a moment, looking down at them, recognising the old insecurity and worry in them, for he had felt it so many times himself. His grin widened. "Somebody dead?"

"Us," the whittler said, "if we don't get some grass. He snapped his jack-knife shut and stood up, a short, stocky man with a round, friendly face and worried eyes. "What are we gonna do, Wayne?" he said.

"Get some grass," Wayne Hardisty said. "What else?"

The other man continued to sit and stare at his folded hands. He was a man in his early thirties—only a few years older than Wayne. He said, "When? I've got enough hay left to feed my cows another week." He looked up suddenly. "It's one thing to be stubborn, Wayne, but there's a time when you got to be sensible. Brod Manwaring has got us where he wants us. He's got grass, and we've got to have it."

Wayne Hardisty felt a mild anger, but it wasn't anger toward the man who, Wayne knew, would overcharge them outrageously for grass. It was anger toward himself and this place, toward a childhood of never quite enough and a youth of less, toward a day when he had known for sure that he loved a girl and had listened to his pride tell him, *You haven't got enough to offer her.* He said, "All right, we'll lease Beaver Creek. But we don't have to take the first offer Brod Manwaring makes without even telling him we know he's robbing us."

"All we'll get is the satisfaction of telling him," Lee Leatherman, the whittler, said.

Wayne grinned. "It'll be worth something to hear Brod beller.

"Depends on your idea of fun, I guess," Bob Faull said. "All I can see is we're wastin' time while our cows get hungry. Mike Conaway's got the lease. I say let's sign it."

"Bob here's right," Leatherman said. "We got to look the facts in the face. Bob and

Newt and me have got twice the stock we can handle on our places. We spent every cent we could borrow buying up enough hay to pull 'em through the winter." He held up his hand. "Now keep your dander down, Wayne. I know you did the same. But the fact remains there's two more months we got to feed them cows before your friend Clegg gets his crew out here and starts trailin' his stockers back to Montana. It's them two months we're talkin' about, Wayne. We got to have graze to hold 'em on. That's the facts and there's no sense dodgin' around 'em. That's how me and Bob here see it, and Newt sees it the same."

"Where is Newt?" Wayne asked.

"Doin' what had to be done," Lee said. "He's talkin' to Mike Conaway about leasin' Beaver Creek."

The anger in Wayne was close to the surface, but he held it in check. "I said to stay away from Mike Conaway, didn't I?"

Bob Faull, the man on the box, stood up for the first time and there was exasperation in his voice. "You said that," he said, "but I'm tired of listening to it. I don't know what's between you and Mike Conaway, Wayne, and I don't give a hang. He's always been a gentleman with me and he's got grass to lease."

"Mike Conaway hasn't got any grass," Wayne Hardisty said. "Mike doesn't own Anvil. Brod Manwaring does. If we have to deal with Anvil, we'll go direct to Brod Manwaring, not to his son-in-law. I told you that."

"That sounds kinda funny, coming from you," Lee Leatherman said carefully. "Your own brother's engaged to Brod Manwaring's daughter, ain't he? Why hasn't your brother been able to get a reasonable deal from Brod?"

"Maybe my brother didn't hold his mouth right," Wayne said flatly.

"Look, Wayne," Bob Faull said patiently. "Brod Manwaring's a sick man. If he was to die tomorrow, Mike Conaway would own Anvil, lock, stock and barrel, and damned if maybe it wouldn't be a good thing. I never had no trouble with Mike Conaway and I don't like the way personal feelings between you and him are enterin' into this. Lee and Newt and me have got families to worry about. You aint. If things go smash, you can pick up and leave—"

"Like I did before? "Wayne said meagrely.

There was a hint of embarrassment in Bob

Faull's voice. "I didn't mean that, Wayne. You had a right to go traipsin' over the country if that's what you wanted. There wasn't nothing to hold you here five years ago."

You're right, Wayne thought. There was nothing to hold me. A dad who was proud of being the best sittin' and whittlin' man in Oregon. A ranch that was falling apart at the seams. A brother who didn't care. A girl I couldn't afford. . . .

He forced a reasoning gentleness into his voice. "We won't get anywhere dealing with Mike Conaway, boys," he said. "The price Mike would charge us for graze would knock our profits in the head. You heard his offer. You know it's so."

"We ain't got much choice, Wayne," Lee Leatherman said. "A thousand cows can get plenty hungry in two months."

"Not if we've got Beaver Creek to run 'em on," Wayne said.

"And that's what we're tryin' to do," Faull said. "Lease Beaver Creek. Newt's talkin' to Mike Conaway about it right now."

"He's talking to the wrong man," Wayne said. The stubbornness was there in his voice, but there was more, too. There was something that said that, regardless of what Mike Conaway did, he would still be the wrong man in Wayne Hardisty's book.

"You're gettin' your back up again, Wayne," Lee Leatherman said. "You know danged well we tried to lease that grass from Brod Manwaring two months ago. Your brother Clyde talked to him, didn't he? Did he do us any good? Brod's mean for the sake of being mean. He always has been. Look what he did to your own dad. Practically stole Beaver Creek from your daddy. Why, just the day before your dad died he was telling me—"

"That everybody was out of step except Dad?" Wayne asked.

Lee Leatherman and Bob Faull glanced at their partner and glanced away. Wayne had given them this opportunity to make up a pool herd of stockers to be sold to a Montana buyer. Without Wayne they wouldn't have had the chance at all. So they owed him the courtesy of listening to his ideas, but they were obviously getting tired of it. When Wayne Hardisty made up his mind to something he could be as stubborn as old Brod Manwaring himself.

Lee Leatherman shrugged his shoulders and expelled his breath in an exaggerated sigh. "All right, damn it," he said. "One more day won't kill us, I guess. We can try talking to Brod again if that's what you want. I'll tell your brother Clyde to go see him."

"I'll talk to Brod myself this time," Wayne said.

Bob Faull cracked the knuckles of his hands and swallowed noisily. There was growing anger in his eyes. "Ain't your personal affairs gettin' a little thick in this, Wayne?"

Wayne started to answer, then checked himself. He touched his split lip with the back of his hand. "No, Faull, they're not," he said.

"I know you and Clyde have been wranglin', Wayne," Faull said. "Damned if I'll stick my head in the sand and say I don't know it. Hell, everybody knows it. That happens sometimes between brothers. But we're all in this thing together and I ain't gonna stand by and see personal feelings take bread out of my mouth. Clyde is practically part of the Manwaring family. If anybody is gonna talk to Brod it ought to be Clyde."

There was no change in Wayne Hardisty's expression. "I'll talk to Brod this time," he said. He turned abruptly and nearly collided with the stableman, who had been standing there in the doorway, listening.

Pete said, "Five years of driftin' didn't teach you a thing, Hardisty. You're as bull-headed as ever. I'm surprised you give in enough to come back."

Wayne looked at Pete and the grin came easily. "If my dad had kept on whittling instead of dying and leaving me half of what used to be a ranch, I wouldn't have come back, Pete." He reached into his pocket and took out a silver dollar and tossed it to Pete. "Buy yourself and my partners in there a drink. You all look like you could use it."

He swung easily into the saddle and turned the bay gelding down the slope.

The livery stable stood on high ground, and riding down from it Wayne could see the whole of the little settlement of Three Rivers, and he gave it the glance of a man who had seen it too many times and grown tired of it. He knew the town as he knew the back of his hand, and he knew the country that lay around it even better. He had built a lot of dreams in this town, but it wasn't a place for dreams. So he had left it, five years ago, taking his dreams with him. His father's death had brought him back. If he still had his dreams he didn't call them such, for a man of twenty-six has different names for dreams than a man of twenty-one.

A girl can grow tired of waiting and the things a man sees along the trail can hammer the softness from him. . . . He tried to whistle but his split lip and the rain got in the way. A half-dozen old acquaintances glanced at him and went about their business, leaving the feel of gossip in the damp air. *It's all over town,* Wayne thought. *If they think Clyde and I fought over Ruth Manwaring, let 'em think it. Ruth and Clyde know better; the rest don't matter.*

He was almost to the town when he saw Mike Conaway round the corner of a building and start up the hill toward the livery stable. Newton, Wayne's other partner, was with Mike. Wayne reined up immediately and waited, letting them come to him. Wayne looked at Mike and thought, *I couldn't leave here if I wanted to. I'd have to know for sure, Mike. . . .*

Mike Conaway was close now, a handsome man in his late twenties, a man with a quick smile, a ready friendliness. He grinned at Wayne and said, "You looking for Newt and me? Sorry if we held you up. We stopped off for a drink. A man bargains better with a drink in his belly."

"That so?" Wayne said. "You figure on making a bargain, do you, Mike?"

There was an immediate tension between the two men. Newt stepped into the breach quickly. "Mike's willing to work out a deal for us on Beaver Creek grass, Wayne."

"You'd be wasting your time, Mike," Wayne Hardisty said. "I'll go talk to Brod about it."

There was a quick flush of anger in Mike Conaway's cheeks and it was not the anger of the moment but a smouldering, deep-seated thing that went back a long way. Mike said, "Look, Hardisty. Ever since you came back here I've tried to get along with you."

"Why bother, Mike?" Wayne said levelly. "We both tried it a few years ago in Wyoming, didn't we? It didn't work out then; it won't now."

Newton stood there a moment, glancing from Mike to Wayne, then he turned and hurried on up the hill. Whatever it was between these two, it was a personal thing, Newton figured. He wanted no part of it.

Mike said, "Why don't you get off my back, Hardisty?"

"Then you'd get off of mine?" Wayne said. "I told you I'd tried to get along with you."

For a moment Wayne looked at Mike Conaway and felt the memory of old friendship, the memory of carefree days and nights and a hundred trails ridden together, drifting from nowhere. Then he thought of a half-breed Indian girl, and he felt the old sickness that he knew would be with him for ever. "Too bad I came back, Mike," Wayne said quietly. "You didn't think I ever would, did you?"

"Why would I give a damn?" Mike said.

"I don't know, Mike," Wayne said. "Why do you?"

The anger was a dark flush in Mike Conaway's cheeks. "You don't believe in anything, do you, Wayne?" Mike said.

"Have you ever done anything to make me believe in you, Mike?"

Mike Conaway had magnificent control of his emotions. His shoulders slumped and he was a man grown tired—tired of the memory of old mistakes, tired of fighting. . . . "I guess I don't blame you, Wayne," he said finally. "I guess it would look bad." Mike jerked his head up suddenly and his eyes were bright. "Damn it, I'm in love with my wife. Is that what you want me to say?"

For just a moment Wayne felt a touch of friendship, and then it was gone. "Tell me five years from now, Mike," Wayne Hardisty said. "I'll still be around." He reined his horse on immediately and he could feel Mike Conaway's anger pressing against him—it was as if the air was charged with it. *Leave it alone, Hardisty,* Wayne thought to himself. *It's over and done with. So Mike Conaway lived with an Indian girl for a while. Maybe he killed her to get rid of her. Someone did. But you'll never know for sure and no man will ever prove it and all talking about the dead can do now is hurt the living. Leave it alone.*

He rode into the town and now his thoughts were back to the errand that had brought him here, and this too was something he didn't want to do, but it was something that couldn't be ignored. *What's the matter with me?* he wondered. *Why do I ride trouble this way?*

For a moment he felt the old urge to drift along, the impatience to be out of a place, and he was actually sorry he had come back. He should have given his share of the inherited, rundown ranch to his brother Clyde as he had originally intended. If Clyde had mismanaged it and lost it, what difference would it have made? Clyde, like Mike Conaway, would soon be a Manwaring, and a Manwaring had no worries. . . .

He rode on, knowing there was no turning back, knowing he really didn't want to turn back. Five years of drifting had settled nothing in his mind; maybe standing still would. A man would never know until he tried it, and there came a time when a man had to know. And standing still meant taking a stand. . . . He rode directly through the town, looking neither to right nor left.

CHAPTER 2

A FEW YARDS beyond the town he turned into a muddy, well-rutted lane and went past a clutter of small cattle pens. A dozen steers of mixed brands huddled wetly against the fence of one of the corrals. He went past the pens and at the end of the lane came to a dilapidated, unpainted building, set on high stilts, its back projecting out over the now raging Fish Creek. Wooden steps led up to a door marked "Office". Wayne dismounted and left his horse ground-tied. He climbed the steps and entered the office of Rudy Effinger's slaughterhouse.

Glancing casually around the empty office, he pushed open a thick, sawdust-insulated door and went into the storage room. A half-dozen dressed beeves hung from travelling hooks on a metal monorail. Rudy Effinger was scrubbing out the place with a stiff-bristle, square broom. He looked up and saw Hardisty and he stood the broom carefully in the corner.

Effinger was a thick, short man with a dark face and no apparent neck. He wore rubber boots and a long, blood-stained rubber apron. "I was expecting your brother," Effinger said.

Hardisty leaned his shoulder against the door frame, a big man, raw-boned, pleasantly homely. His blond hair, three months uncut, stood up in rebellious duck tails where the collar of his slicker met his neck. He looked steadily at Rudy Effinger. "He won't be here, Rudy," Wayne said.

Effinger's dark eyes moved swiftly across the hanging carcasses. "He better be," he said. "Your brother owes me some money. We worked out a deal. It's all settled."

Wayne shook his head slowly. "No, Effinger."

Effinger didn't back down. "A man has to pay his poker debts in this country, Hardisty," he said. "I went a long ways, offering to let your brother pay off with beef."

"You went too far, Rudy," Wayne said softly. "You're not going to be paid. Not in

17

beef or any other way. Not for that kind of a game."

"You want to say that plainer, Hardisty?" There was a deadly note of assurance in Rudy Effinger's voice.

"Sure," Wayne said. "It was a rigged game. It was a marked deck. My brother was drunk. You and your pal Calvin figured it was a way to get some beef cheap without stealing it like you usually do. You were wrong. That plain enough, Effinger?"

The corner of Effinger's mouth twitched. He was a man who liked to push things as far as he could, but he always left himself an alley of escape. "Your brother signed an IOU, Hardisty," Effinger said. "It says on that paper I got six beeves coming to me. I mean to have 'em."

There was more tiredness than anger in Wayne now. "My brother changed his mind," Wayne said.

"I won't bluff, Hardisty," Rudy Effinger said. "Maybe you play wet nurse for your brother. I don't. If he can't afford to lose, he shouldn't gamble. You think this is the first time? You been gone five years. I'll tell you something, Hardisty—"

"Shut up," Wayne said quietly. "I didn't ask you anything. I don't want any answers.

Just don't try to pick up those six steers. You won't get 'em." He turned abruptly and started to walk away. Effinger's voice stopped him.

"You ain't convinced me of nothing, Hardisty," Effinger said. "You deliver those steers by tomorrow or I'll be out after 'em."

The memory of last night's anger, his fight with his brother over this gambling debt, the worry over Mike Conaway, rose in Wayne's throat. He turned and started back and he saw Effinger's eyes widen. He reached out and caught Effinger by the front of the apron and jerked him close. "Listen to me, Rudy," Wayne said, "and listen close. You fool with me and I'll hang you by the throat on one of your own meat hooks." He shoved hard, slamming the butcher against the wall, then turned immediately, knowing he had to get out of here. He went back through the office and out into the rain, leaving the office door open behind him.

He mounted his horse and rode rapidly out of town in the opposite direction from the road that had brought him here. The sleeplessness of last night burned his eyes and dried his mouth. There was a growing feeling of loneliness on him that was as oppressive as the weather. He tried to shake it and found he couldn't.

He knew as well as he knew his own name that Mike Conaway had been instrumental in getting Clyde Hardisty into that crooked poker game. Quietly, bit by bit, Mike Conaway was doing everything in his power to break up the engagement of Clyde Hardisty and Ruth Manwaring. Mike had no intentions of sharing the Manwaring ranch with anyone, least of all with a Hardisty. Wayne knew it was so, but he could never prove it, any more than he could prove anything else against Mike, nor any more than he could excuse his own brother's weakness. He knew Mike Conaway too well to think he could prove anything against him. Too well, and yet not well enough.

He remembered back to the days when he and Mike were saddle-tramp friends, working a spell, moving on. You looked for sociability and companionship in a man in those days; you didn't ask his pedigree. And with dreams on your mind you talked a lot— talked about home, the biggest ranch in your part of the country, even exaggerating a bit. You talked about Brod Manwaring who owned that ranch, and you made a joke about Brod Manwaring having two daughters and no sons and you said some lucky waddie would marry one of those girls and inherit everything. . . . "That's my idea of good living," Mike Conaway said, and it was only a joke. Around a fire with no money in your pocket and a half-drained bottle between you, you talked.

Wayne rode on up the well-rutted road that led to Anvil headquarters, though increasingly sizable bunches of Anvil cattle. His thoughts shifted to Brod Manwaring now, and he found it impossible to think of Brod wasting away in bed. He remembered Brod always as a big man on a big horse, speaking with a big voice—a man who was soundly hated because he was a successful man. And he thought of himself as a kid, a skinny tow-headed boy with bare feet on the bottom rail of a zigzag fence, his chin resting on the top rail. He remembered himself standing there in the hot sun, standing there a long time, watching a herd of Brod Manwaring's Anvil cattle being trailed north towards The Dalles, and he remembered how the calling mystery that was the Columbia River grabbed at a small boy's stomach and made his head swim with visions of the great gorge and the mystical city of Portland and the endless sea that lay yonder somewhere. Somewhere. . . . He remembered the animal heat of the herd sweeping against him, engulfing him. And he remembered thinking even then as he watched the great man on the great horse becoming a vision behind the film of dust, thinking, some day I'll be like you, Mr. Manwaring. Some day I'll drive a herd and see the river and the town and the ocean beyond. I don't want to be like my own father: I want to be like you.

The rain stopped momentarily and the low bundles of grey clouds scudded across the landscape treetop high. The road to Anvil lifted through rolling hills and past thickets of juniper, freshly pungent with their grey-green odour after the rain. This was a fine ranch, this Anvil. This was the kind of ranch Mike Conaway used to say he'd marry some day. Sitting around a camp fire with a half-empty bottle between them, Mike used to talk to Wayne about marrying a ranch. And Mike had married a ranch—a run-down affair with a few cows and a few horses, owned by a half-breed Indian girl, a girl who was brutally murdered by a party or parties unknown, as the authorities put it. "I got to get out of here," Mike Conaway said at the funeral. "There's too many memories. . . ."

Wayne hadn't seen Mike again; he didn't miss him. Something had died between Mike and Wayne, died with the Indian girl. A thing called respect, the anchor that holds friendship together. He didn't see Mike again until after old man Hardisty's death. Wayne had come back, arriving too late for the funeral, and he had found Mike, married to Mercy Manwaring, an impulsive and affectionate girl of seventeen whom Wayne had always looked on as a kid sister.

Wayne drew air deeply into his lungs. I'm no judge of women, he thought. I've proved that. Maybe Mike's right for Mercy. How would I know? And immediately he thought, I'm responsible for Mike being here. I told him about Anvil; I told him about Mercy. It's my responsibility. I'll stay until I do know. . . .

He came to the little stand of timber that rimmed Anvil's horse pasture and rode through it to the outer gate. Dismounting, he unlatched the gate and closed it behind him and led his horse the short distance to the bunkhouse. A hundred old memories of this place, a sense of belonging, lifted his spirits, and as he approached the bunkhouse, a tall, thin, red-headed man, packing a saddle in one hand, a warbag in the other, stamped angrily through the bunkhouse door and glared at the soggy world. The weight of the saddle and the loaded warbag pulled at the man's thin shoulders. He turned around and stared at the door, making a problem of whether he should leave the door open or put down his burden to close it. Seeing the man, all seriousness dropped from Wayne Hardisty's thoughts and amusement found his eyes. He moved on, unnoticed by the red-head, and he spoke casually. "Got a match, Tex?" Wayne asked.

"Sure," the red-head said. He started to put down the saddle, then looked up, saw it was Wayne and said promptly, "You tryin' to get yourself whipped?"

A grin tugged at the corners of Wayne's eyes but he kept his voice serious. He glanced toward an invisible sun and said, "Things have changed. Slowed up some. Brod used to fire you at eight in the morning, didn't he?"

Tex Blanchard had been on Anvil as long back as Wayne could remember. He hadn't changed one iota in appearance in all those years. Tex said, "If he wasn't sick in bed I'd call him outside, I'll tell you that straight. If he figgers he can put a cockleburr under my tail he ain't reckoned with my hind feet."

Tex was a born iconoclast. Nothing had ever been right for him. He grumbled constantly and found fault with everything from the range bulls to the way the boss's daughters wore their hair. But he did his work with more efficiency than any three men and his loyalty had earned him his right to fight with the boss. For all of twenty-five years Brod Manwaring had fired Tex at least once a day. Wayne shrugged and said, "Well, you didn't figure this job would be permanent anyway, did you?"

"If it hadn't been for him bellyin' down to me and whinin' like a pup I'd a never stayed in the first place," Tex said. "This time it won't do him no good."

Wayne laughed silently. Tex rarely got further than the bunkhouse door when he quit, but quit he must. It was his way of keeping his independence. "Must have been real serious," Wayne said. "What was it about?"

A sheepish grin nearly closed Tex Blanchard's eyes. "I forget," he said, "but it was a good one."

"You and Brod ought to keep a tally book, Tex," Wayne said. "That way you could remember what you fight about."

Tex squinted one eye and spat at his toe. "I wouldn't get sassy with me if I was you,

Hardisty," he said. He stalked back into the bunkhouse and Wayne heard him throw his gear heavily on the floor. *There's a smart man,* Wayne thought. *He knows how to get things out of his system.* He was still chuckling when he tied his horse to a porch post at the main house.

CHAPTER
3

THE HOUSE WAS a long affair that had been added to from time to time, so that nearly every one of its eight rooms opened directly off the long porch. Wayne turned left and started to walk down three doors to the room he knew was Brod Manwaring's combination bedroom and office. A girl's voice said, "What's the matter? Am I poison?"

He turned abruptly and saw Ruth Manwaring there at the far end of the porch. She was dressed for the rain and she was carrying a bucket full of eggs. The grin reached the corners of Wayne's wide mouth as he saw the oversize yellow slicker and the slouch rain hat the girl wore. It wasn't a pretty outfit but it was a practical one. Ruth was like that.

26

Looking at his future sister-in-law Wayne felt a fleeting sadness, like the sadness of an old man looking back, knowing the old days were lived through and done with. He said soberly, "I don't know whether I want to talk to you or not, knowing your disposition. Those eggs would make mighty good throwing ammunition."

"When I throw something at you it will be harder than an egg," she said. She came up on to the porch and set down the heavy bucket and started rubbing the palm of her hand where the pail had bitten into the flesh.

She was a solidly built girl with chestnut hair and expressive brown eyes. There was a dark mellowness to her skin, as if the long winter had failed to erase last summer's tan. She had a stubborn chin and her nose was high-bridged, straight. Her dark eyebrows and lashes gave her eyes depth and softness. She said, "The coffee pot's on."

He was immediately conscious of his split lip and bruised cheek, and he knew if he lingered to have a cup of coffee with her the conversation would have to turn to Clyde. His desire for a moment of relaxation overcame his reluctance. "Haven't had any of your coffee for quite a spell now," he drawled. "Might sample some to see if you've learned to make it yet."

"After that swill you make, how would you know?" she said.

Wayne chuckled, a feeling of well-being and relaxation growing in him. "Take it easy now," he said. "If that chip on your shoulder gets wet it might swell and weigh you down."

"You'd know about such things," she said promptly.

She took off the rain hat and tossed it on the porch and kicked her way out of the over-size rubber boots. She stood there on the porch then in her stocking feet and he found himself surprised at her size. He had always thought of her as a tall girl. Memory played funny tricks on a man. He watched her as she shrugged out of the slicker and hung it on a nail at the side of the door. Her hair, damp from the rain, was tightly curled, tousled and unruly. She had that same physical adaptability to weather Wayne Hardisty had. Whether it was a scorching summer day or a howling winter blizzard. Ruth Manwaring managed to look as if the weather itself had tapped a spring of vitality in her. She said, "I really don't want your company. I'm just in hopes someone will see us together. Gossip about the love life of the Manwaring sisters has died down some and things are getting dull."

She was joking, but there was a trace of irritation in her voice, too. The town had made much of the fact that Ruth, now engaged to Clyde Hardisty, had once been more than a little interested in Wayne. Mercy's sudden marriage to Mike Conway had added delicious spice to the gossip. The motherless and somewhat unconventional daughters of the country's biggest rancher had always made good table conversation.

Wayne reached out and picked up the heavy bucket of eggs. "They do talk, don't they?" he said. "I'll tote this in for you."

"You could have come out to the barn and got it instead of standing there teasing poor Tex," she said.

"I saved your top hand for you," Wayne said. "He was right set on quitting."

She laughed honestly and he thought, *It was worth the trip to hear that.*

"I think his daily fight with Tex is one thing that keeps Dad going," she said. She opened the door and they stepped into the ample kitchen. Closing the door, she said, "I'll get some shoes."

"Why?" he said. "You think I haven't seen you bare-footed before?"

She laughed again. "Remember old Fuzzy Ears? The teacher we had in the third grade? He said I couldn't come to school until I wore shoes and acted like a lady." He saw a hint of the old devilment in her eyes. "Do you suppose my life will be blighted because I missed a month of the third grade?"

Mine was, at the time, he remembered. *There wasn't anybody left in school big enough for me to fight with.*

He shook his head. "You were a gawky somebody along about then."

"You always say the nicest things," she said. "Do you intend to hold that bucket of eggs all day?"

He set the bucket down immediately and felt a quick embarrassment which he knew she noticed. He hadn't even been aware that he was holding the bucket.

The room was long and wide and the pine-panelled walls, finished natural, had a warm mellowness that was comfortably satisfying after the outside weather. She went to one of the huge cupboards that lined a complete wall and reached down two of the thick mugs the men used for coffee. She put the cups on the table and took the pot from the mammoth wood range and poured the cups full. Only then did Wayne sit down. He took off his hat and tossed it to the floor by the door, unbuttoned his slicker and pushed it open. She glanced at him and said, "You better take your coat off. You'll be cold when you go outside."

"I'll warm up fast," he said. "I came to talk to your dad about leasing Beaver Creek from him."

She looked up quickly and he knew she was thinking. *You should have talked to Mike. Mike is running Anvil now.* He knew she was thinking that, but instead she said, "You've always wanted Beaver Creek for your own, haven't you, Wayne?"

"I had it once," he said. He corrected himself. "My dad did, anyway."

She said, "Are you being bitter?"

A wry grin lifted one corner of his mouth. "I don't rightly see how I could be, Ruth," he said. "If I had been in Brod's shoes I would have foreclosed on it six months sooner."

"I'm afraid you and Dad are a lot alike, Wayne."

"I'll take that as a compliment."

She sat down at the table, as much at ease as if a visit such as this was an ordinary thing instead of something that had happened with increasing rarity since Wayne had returned to the Three Rivers country. It hadn't been a rarity once, Wayne remembered. He thought back to a time when only his pride had stood between himself and this girl. When he glanced up he saw her looking at him and her deep brown eyes were serious. With characteristic impulsiveness she reached across the table and laid her hand on his hand. "We've always been frank with each other, Wayne," she said. "What was it about?"

He felt an immediate discomfort. He had known he would have to answer this question about his fight with his brother sooner or later. He shrugged. "Clyde and I are brothers," he said. "You've got a sister. Didn't you ever fight with her?"

"Is that all the answer I'm going to get?"

"That's all there is."

"All right, Wayne," she said tiredly. "Let's talk about cows. That ought to be safe enough."

And you'll be closer to the truth than you were before, he thought. He pushed back from the table and stretched his legs, first one and then the other, then took the thick mug and cradled it in his big hands. "We're up to our ears in cows," he said. "Me and Leatherman and Newton and Faull. Long on cows, short on feed."

He allowed himself a sigh. "Seemed like a good idea when I talked the boys into it," he said. "Big outfits in Wyoming and Montana are crying for stockers."

"Why Oregon cattle?" she said.

"They winter better," Wayne said. "It gets cold back there."

She let the silence run, then said, "Suppose you can't reach an agreement with Dad on Beaver Creek?"

"In that case," he said, "I reckon we'll have to teach our cows to eat rocks."

"You're lucky in one respect," she said. "Dad's in a good mood these days." She seemed to be looking way off into the past and there was a dreaminess in her eyes. "He's dying happy, Wayne," she said softly. "He's got someone to carry on with Anvil." She smiled. "It isn't much of a compliment to me and Mercy finding out how much Dad really wanted a son, is it?"

"If he hadn't had daughters he wouldn't have had son-in-laws," Wayne said.

Once she had been uneasy around Wayne, careful of what she said. There was no need any longer. He had gone away without asking her what she had once hoped he would ask her. Unexpressed emotions can die in five years. *And Clyde was available,* she thought, and immediately hated herself for that unfairness. She said, "You haven't any use for Mike, have you?"

"I haven't any use for snow either," he said. "It snows anyway."

She got up and refilled their cups and they sat there a long time, sipping at the thick mugs. The rain fell with soft intensity, a steady whisper on the shake roof of the kitchen. His eyes became serious. "I picked up a little wedding present for Mercy," he said. "I'm only six months late. Mercy and Mike living in the white house?" Everyone always referred to the two-storey frame that stood just beyond the main house as "the white house". It had formerly been used as a foreman's house.

"You wouldn't have needed to buy Mercy a present," she said. "You had one ready-made."

He knew what she was going to say. He wished she wouldn't say it.

"Your friendship to Mike." There was a new intentness in her voice. "Why, Wayne? You've known Mike longer than any of us. He came directly to us for a job, saying he was a friend of yours. Heaven knows he's tried hard enough to patch up whatever it is between you."

He shifted uneasily, annoyed that the conversation had taken this turn, knowing it couldn't have taken any other. "Let's just say it's my fault," he said.

She looked at him a long time and said, "That wasn't like you to say that, Wayne."

What is like me? he wondered. *What am I like, really?* He shrugged and said, "I couldn't think of a better answer."

"Couldn't or wouldn't?" she said

"All right," he said. "Didn't, then."

Again she gave him her steady look. "You've changed; Wayne," she said quietly. "Does wandering around the country do that to a man?"

Maybe it does, he thought. *Maybe seeing the rottenness in someone you like does it.* He thought wearily, *Why don't I tell her?* and knew he never would.

He stood up then, knowing they were approaching dangerous ground, resentful of the things that had spoiled this moment together. "Is it all right if I go see your dad now?" he asked.

She glanced at the wall clock and said, "You'd better wait a while, Wayne. He'll be

35

taking a nap now. You might as well wait here."

"You got things to do," he said. "I'll go on out and beat Tex at a game of crib." He knew their conversation would only become increasingly unpleasant and he didn't want it that way. *Running away again,* he thought wryly.

She got up and moved between him and the door and stood there as if barring his way. She said, "I know Clyde lost some money in a poker game. Mike told me."

Mike would, Wayne thought. He said, "A man has to blow off steam now and then."

"I know that," she said. She looked squarely into his eyes. "I don't look for perfection, Wayne. It saves me a lot of heart-aches."

He stood there close to her, looking down at her, then reached past her and turned the door-knob. "You're a smart girl, Ruth," he said. "Any man is entitled to one mistake. Maybe some day I'll learn that." He reached down with a swift, smooth movement and picked up his hat. "It was good coffee," he said. He stepped through the door and crossed the porch and walked directly to the bunkhouse. *But when does it stop being a mistake and start being a pattern?* he wondered.

How many times do you let a snake bite before you figure he's dangerous?

Mike Conaway left the unsuccessful meeting with Leatherman, Faull and Newton and rode out toward Rudy Effinger's slaughterhouse. Rudy had a contract to supply meat to the camps of the Big Pine Lumber Company. The camps would be opening soon and Rudy would be needing beef, and in that need, Mike saw a way to pick up a little pocket money. Old Brod Manwaring, for all his friendliness, was still holding a tight rein on Anvil's purse strings, and that fact was a growing irritation to Mike Conaway. He wasn't a man who liked being broke; he liked even less going to his wife and asking for a handout every time he wanted to go to town. It had gotten to the point where lack of money was beginning to irritate Mike as much as Wayne Hardisty irritated him.

Riding up to Effinger's slaughterhouse, Mike let that worry fleet across his mind, then put it aside. He swung down and went up the steps to Effinger's office, pausing at the door to shake the water from his slicker. Pushing through the door, he caught Effinger pacing back and forth across the room, a picture of smouldering anger. Rudy paused and said, "Oh, Conaway. Come out of the weather."

A second man was sitting at Effinger's desk, tilted back in a swivel chair. He was cleaning his nails with a pocket-knife and now he glanced at Mike Conaway and grinned. "Wet out?" he asked.

"For the past month," Mike Conaway said. "Damn this weather."

"Nice part of being single," the man at the desk said. "If the weather gets tiresome, you can ride away from it." He snapped the knife shut and took his feet from the desk.

He was a totally thin man. His lips were thin and his sandy hair was thin. He had a smile that was so perpetual it had etched itself deeply into every line of his face, and yet it was a smile with no warmth or meaning to it. His name was Lorry Calvin, and he had drifted into Three Rivers two years ago, not saying where he was from, not particularly inviting anyone to ask. He was friendly, but he avoided making friends, and with the exception of Rudy Effinger, no one knew much about him. Whether he had bought into a partnership with Effinger or was merely an employee, no one knew for sure. Calvin and Effinger never discussed their business with anyone but themselves.

There was a feeling of tension in the room, heightened by the dark scowl on Effinger's face. Noting it, Mike said, "Am I busting into a private discussion?"

Lorry turned the swivel chair and let his lazy gaze drift to Mike Conaway. He moved slowly and smoothly, like a huge, tawny cat, just awakening from a sleep. The perpetual grin widened slightly. "Not at all, Mike. What's on your mind? Another poker game?"

Mike felt immediately uncomfortable. He didn't like Calvin. He didn't like the free way Calvin talked to him, always as if there were some sort of conspiracy between himself and Mike. He didn't like the look in Calvin's eyes, the veiled references Calvin always made to a past, making them in a way that said plainly he figured Mike Conaway, too, had a past. Mike's mouth felt dry. He said, "The way it looks, I'll have a few head of beef I can spare you."

Rudy shot Calvin a quick glance. "Always interested," Rudy said. "If the price is right."

Mike half turned, ignoring Calvin, making it obvious that he was talking to Effinger. "Whatever the going price is," Mike said. "Could you use six head?"

"Rudy's gonna get six," Lorry Calvin said. "A man owes 'em to him."

"Shut up, Lorry," Effinger said. He gave Mike a knowing smile. "Sure, Conaway," he said. "I can always use some beef." He glanced quickly at Calvin, as if looking for support, tried to meet Mike's eyes and failed. "I'm playing it pretty close to the belt on that Big Pines contract," he said. "Puts me in a spot where I have to buy as cheap as I can. . . ."

He was being mildly blackmailed, Mike knew, and it was exactly what he had expected. The mere fact that he was offering to sell Anvil beef to Rudy Effinger was an admission that he was doing it behind Brod's back. In addition, there had been Mike's willingness to get Clyde Hardisty into a crooked poker game with these two. Mike didn't like it, but he liked being broke less. *Make the best of it,* he told himself. *Another couple of months and you'll be set.* He grinned and said, "You're a couple of nice boys, you two. You'd rob your own grandmother."

"What the devil," Lorry Calvin said. "What's a few head of beef to Brod Manwaring?"

"I can do what I damn please with Anvil

beef," Mike Conaway said. "I'm running Anvil."

"Sure, Mike," Lorry Calvin said. "Sure you are." He stood up then, and now the slackness was gone from him and it was as if all the tendons in his body had come to attention at once, pulling him together. He wore no gun belt, and yet the manner of his standing suggested a gun. He grinned at Mike and said, "I'm gonna collect six steers from Wayne Hardisty." He stood there, grinning, obviously expecting Mike to make something of that.

Mike felt a quick resentment. "Don't tell me," he said. "I don't give a damn about Wayne Hardisty."

"Don't you?" Calvin said.

"Why should I?"

"You'd know that," Calvin said. "I wouldn't. All I know is, he rides yuh." Lorry looked up with that quick grin. "Maybe Hardisty figures if you drive a herd of Anvil stockers to Montana you'll take the pay-off and forget to come back," Lorry said.

Mike felt the colour drain from his face. He knew Lorry was just talking. It was his way. But the uncanny way Lorry Calvin had of picking so close to the truth was completely unnerving. It was almost as if Calvin, recognising one of his own kind in Mike, could read and even anticipate Mike's every thought. The anger rose swiftly in Mike. He said, "You're damned free with your remarks, Lorry." He took two steps forward, then stopped.

Lorry Calvin hadn't made a move. He was still standing there, still smiling. And Mike felt as if Lorry Calvin had jammed a gun against his stomach. "I was just joking," Lorry said.

"A damn poor joke," Mike said gruffly, saving what dignity he could. He turned and started through the door. "I'll let you know about the beef," he muttered across his shoulder to Effinger. He wanted out of here.

Later, riding home to Anvil, Mike Conaway thought about what Lorry Calvin had said. It didn't mean anything, Mike assured himself. It was not secret that he had planned to drive a herd of Anvil stockers to Montana. It was good business. A man would be a fool to pass it up. Even Brod Manwaring had agreed to that. It was like Lorry to make a remark about stealing Brod's cattle. Lorry's mind ran that way.

Mike Conaway turned his coat collar up against the rain. The miserable, endless rain. The same rain that had held up his departure a month already. The same damn rain his wife Mercy liked. . . .

Just a joke, he told himself again. *But I don't like you thinking it, Lorry. And I'm tired of having Wayne Hardisty watching every move I make. I'm tired of Oregon, tired of being broke. I'm tired of a lot of things. . . .*

He rode on, his eyes fixed moodily on the bobbing head of his horse. He thought of his wife, Mercy, and was immediately angry. *I'm tiredest of all of you,* he decided wearily.

CHAPTER
4

SPRAWLED IN A CHAIR at Anvil's bunkhouse table, with a greasy deck of cards between himself and the grumbling Tex Blanchard, Wayne Hardisty caught the nostalgic feel of other rainy afternoons and other days of lazy companionship when a man could drift and not worry about tomorrow. A growing pile of brown cigarette butts in a pound coffee can testified to Tex Blanchard's increasing irritation. Wayne counted his points in a drawling monotone. "Fifteen two, fifteen four. . . ." He started pegging off the holes in the cribbage board.

"I don't mind your outright cheatin' so much," Tex muttered, "but when you start lopin' off them holes four at a time. . . ."

"How would you know?" Wayne said. "Why don't you give up and get yourself some specs? You afraid the widow Clinton might find out you're eighty-seven instead of the fifty you claim to be?"

"Hah!" Tex snorted.

Wayne finished pegging off the holes, completing the game. "Why don't you get married, Tex?" he said. "Won't she have you?"

"Why don't you get the hell out of here and give me a chance to air the place out?" Tex said.

Wayne glanced at the alarm clock sitting on a shelf above Tex's bunk, stretched his arms and yawned widely. "You figger Brod's awake by now?"

"How would I know?" Tex said. "I don't pussyfoot around waitin' for him to wake up. If I got something to Brod I go say it to him. If he don't want to listen I hold him down and make him listen."

"Brod that weak now?" Wayne said. "He must be sicker than I figured. Wish I was brave like you instead of so doggone smart." He glanced at the cribbage board. "Pay me."

"For what?"

"Two bits. I won. Pay me."

"I don't remember makin' no such bet."

"I do. Pay me or I'll take it out of your hide."

"You and how many cousins?" Tex said. He reached into his pocket, grumbling, took out a quarter and flung it on the table. "I'd rather pay than hear you whine," he said.

Wayne glanced through the murky window. "It's quit raining," he observed.

"Damned if you can take credit for that," Tex said.

Wayne picked up his slicker from the back of the chair where he had tossed it. He swung it around with deliberate carelessness so that its moist folds draped themselves over Tex's head. "Pardon me all to hell!" Wayne said.

Tex clawed off the slicker and made a dive at Wayne just as Wayne cleared the door and slammed it in Tex's face. He stood there a moment, holding the door closed, listening to Tex's wild threats of bodily harm, feeling Tex tugging against the inward opening door. Suddenly Wayne released his grip. The door opened and he heard Tex crash against the table. He ran then, dodging just in time to avoid a boot that Tex hurled after him.

Damned if I wouldn't trade places with you, Tex, he caught himself thinking.

The freshness of the after-rain lay over everything. A rooster crowed and Ruth's chickens were especially noisy. *A sign it will clear up,* Wayne thought as he walked across to the main house and up on to the porch, and immediately he was thinking of Mike Conaway. He walked down along to the room that was Brod Manwaring's combination bedroom and office. He rapped on the door and heard Brod's thin voice commanding him to come in.

The room was large and cluttered and wholly a man's room. It was the one part of the house Brod Manwaring had saved as his own when his wife was alive and later while his daughters were growing up. From the battered roll-top desk to the heavy four-poster bed it was all man and all Brod Manwaring. The only thing wrong now was the medicinal smell that clung to everything.

Brod Manwaring was propped up in the bed. Wayne hid his startled surprise when he saw how much the old man had failed in a scant two months, but as cleverly as he hid it, Brod saw it. Brod said, "Maybe I don't look it, Hardisty, but I'm a long ways from dead. Whatever you want, the answer is no."

"Good," Wayne said. "I was gonna offer you a quart of whiskey."

"Like hell," Brod Manwaring said. "You wouldn't give a man the sweat out of your saddle blanket unless you expected to get his horse in return."

"Would you?" Wayne asked.

"No," Brod said. There was a twinkle in his frosty blue eyes. He was obviously pleased that Wayne had come to see him; he was trying hard not to show it. He said, "What brings you here besides the idle curiosity of wanting to see an old man die?"

"Not your company," Wayne said. "That's for sure." He hooked out a chair and sat down and flipped his hat on to the bed as if he intended to stay a while. "I brought Mercy a wedding present," he said.

"Tell her about it," Brod said. "Not me."

The old man's eyes were keenly inquisitive in a pinched face that had turned the colour of old parchment. He had a scraggly, white moustache that drooped down around the lines of a bony, square chin. His cheeks were sunken, making his nose sharp and beaklike, and his blue-veined hands, lying on top of the coverlet, were thin claws. He had been a brute of a man at one time; now he was a bony frame with only his spirit holding him together.

"You look like hell, Brod," Wayne said.

"You and Tex are the only ones with guts enough to say so," Brod said. He grinned. "How's things in town? Everybody got bets down on when I'll cash in?"

"Wouldn't know, Brod," Wayne said. "It's the first time I been through town in two months. If they're betting, though, I'd like to get in on it. There's enough meanness in you to carry you another ten years."

Brod Manwaring managed a soft laugh. "Too bad you and the boys didn't get that lease you were counting on."

"Those things happen."

"Puts you against a hard rock, don't it?"

"Unless we get some grass, it does," Wayne said.

"So you got to have some grass." Wayne saw Brod watching him closely, a sharp old man in spite of his sickness, a man who had built an empire by keeping sentiment out of business. He was a man who had found success and found it a lonely place, but he still had no time for failure. *How should I go about it?* Wayne wondered to himself. *Will I say, "Please Mr. Manwaring?"* He settled back in his chair and stretched his legs, first one and then the other in that manner he had, and his eyes were serious. You didn't ever get any place crawling to Brod Manwaring. Wayne knew. No one ever had.

"It make you happy?" Wayne asked.

"Why not?" Brod said. "You had to come to me, didn't you?"

"Not crawling," Wayne said.

"A little crawling might not hurt you," Brod said. He kept darting quick glances at Wayne's face, wise enough to know that the marks on it had been made by fists, respectful enough of another man's privacy not to ask about it. "Did you see Ruth?" he asked suddenly.

"Had a cup of coffee with her," Wayne said.

"Damned if you don't manage to always get something for nothing," Brod said. "You expect to get some grass for nothing?"

"Nope," Wayne said. "I expect to pay for it. But I don't expect to pay ten times what it's worth."

"You want Beaver Creek, don't you?"

"It would do. If the price was right."

Brod Manwaring was thoughtful a long time. He looked at his thin hands on the covers and built a steeple with his fingers. "My son-in-law is running Anvil, Wayne," he said quietly. "You talk to him about Beaver Creek."

"I've talked to Mike," Wayne said. "I don't like his deal."

"I said Mike was running Anvil."

"I expect he is," Wayne said. "It figures. He's your son-in-law."

"What's between you two, Wayne?" Brod asked quietly. Wayne looked at the old man, remembering him as he had once known him, remembering Ruth and Mercy. *I'd accomplish a hell of a lot telling him, wouldn't I?* he thought meagrely. *Like a tattletale kid saying I think Mike wrote nasty words on a fence.* "A lot of people don't like you, Brod," Wayne said. "I don't reckon they ever stop to figure out why exactly."

Brod Manwaring heaved a deep sigh. "What do you expect me to do, Wayne? Throw my own daughter off the place because she married somebody I didn't pick out for her?"

Brod's mention of family affairs, as small as it was, surprised Wayne. He said, "I expect you to do exactly what you're doing, Brod. It's what I'd do if I were in your place."

Brod pushed himself further against the

pillows and there was a sadness in him Wayne had never seen before. For the first time he was an old man, critically ill, an old man at the end of the road long before he was ready to finish his journey. "What happened, Wayne?" Brod asked. "I thought I had it figured once. I thought it would be you and Ruth." The old man was immediately angry, and it was the kind of anger he could conjure up rapidly to cover sentiment.

Wayne laughed. "You and me would have beat each other's heads off with a singletree inside of a week."

Brod sighed deeply and the breath rattled in his bony chest. "We would of, at that," he said. "But we'd a had a hell of a good time doing it." He was suddenly all anger again. He made a hacking sound in his throat. "Well, say your piece. Your pants getting too tight and the pocket rivets starting to dig into your behind? What are you crying about?"

"When you see the tears falling, Brod, I'm crying," Wayne said. "I come to offer you a business proposition. Do you want to lease Beaver Creek to me and my partners or not?"

Even sick in bed there was dignity in Brod

Manwaring and it was a dignity backed by a stubborn-necked pride. He had spent his life convincing people he was right by never backing down from a decision once he had made it. He looked steadily at Wayne Hardisty and said, "I told you, Wayne. My son-in-law is running Anvil. You make your proposition to him, not me."

Wayne stood up and looked down at the emaciated form on the bed. "That your final word, Brod?"

"It was final two months ago," Brod Manwaring said.

"All right, Brod," Wayne said. "If that's it, it's it." He reached out and took his hat from the bed and started toward the door.

Brod Manwaring's reedy voice said, "Wayne?"

Wayne turned his hand on the door-knob. "Yeah, Brod?"

"Mike's doing all right," Brod said. "He's a good cow man. He's taken hold like the place is his own. I like that, Wayne. He'll have his chance."

The anger and disappointment that had been in Wayne fled immediately. He looked at the old man in the bed and saw suddenly that Brod wasn't being stubborn; he was doing the only thing he could do. He couldn't turn the job of running Anvil over to Mike Conaway one day and then turn around and go over Mike's head the next. Wayne said, "All right, Brod. I always told my dad if he wasn't man enough to stand up to you he deserved to be set down. I guess I can take my own preachin'." He managed a grin. "Maybe I'll have to take that job you offered me five years ago."

"It'll always be there for you, Wayne," Brod said. "It always has been." Again that sudden flare of emotion covering anger flushed Brod's face. "You damn bull-headed jackass," he said. "Why didn't you come to me first? What'd you send Clyde for? Did you expect to get something for nothing just because your brother is engaged to my daughter?"

That manoeuvre hadn't been Wayne's idea. It had been Leatherman and Faull and Newton who had dreamed that one up. They might as well have waved a red flag in front of an angry bull. Brod had flared up and set his price right then, and now he was stuck with it, for a decision with Brod— even one made in anger—was still a decision. "I figured you might want to give Clyde a break," Wayne said.

"He'll get his break after he marries

Ruth," Brod said. "Until then he'll stand on his own feet." He glanced quickly at Wayne, and Wayne knew Brod was seeing the split lip, the fist bruises.

Wayne grinned. "Clyde's grown up some since the last time I tried to whip him," he said. "Damned if I didn't have a time of it."

"He should have taken a club to yuh," Brod muttered.

"He did," Wayne said. He left the room, feeling Brod Manwaring's amused glance on his back.

Wayne went back on to the porch and stepped off the end, short-cutting the steps, and walked across the yard to the white house where Mercy and Mike Conaway lived. The aroma of dried apple pie, still hot, seeped out and lay in the damp air. The pies were standing on the sill of an open window. He reached out and took one pie in each hand, then leaned through the window and said, "It was dog-gone nice of you to make these for me, Mercy."

The girl at the stove straightened suddenly. She was small, incredibly pretty, a girl with deep brown eyes and a wealth of gold-red hair. Caught in the middle of baking, she was still as fresh and crisp as an autumn morning. Her lips were full and red, her entire bearing one of energy and exuberant friendliness. She put her hands on her hips and stamped her foot like a little girl, and it was exactly what anyone would have expected her to do. She said, "Wayne Hardisty! You put those pies back in that window right this minute, do you hear?"

"If I didn't hear, I'm deaf," he said. "Only six months married and already you sound like a wife."

She came to the door and threw it wide in a manner that said Mercy Conaway knew no other way to open a door. "Come in here, you big moose," she said. "How are you? How have you been? I've got coffee on the stove. What have you been doing for yourself? Wayne, it's wonderful seeing you!"

"Fine, fine, good, working, thanks," Wayne said. "I guess that answers everything."

"You goof!" she said. "I'm a coffee drinker too," he said.

She looked quickly around the kitchen, a girl who could be surprised with familiar things, and she giggled like a schoolgirl. "Can you imagine me cooking and everything?"

You still think you're playing house, he thought sadly.

She moved the coffee pot on to a hotter stove-lid and got two of her best cups from the cupboard. "Have you seen Ruth?" she asked.

"Mooched a cup of coffee from her too," he said.

"And Dad?"

"Just now."

She looked at him and he saw the worry in her eyes, but she was a girl who felt that if she ignored unpleasantness it would presently go away. She said, "Did any civil words pass between you and Dad?"

"Not one."

"I'm glad you came to see him, Wayne," she said quietly. "He really thinks a lot of you."

He knew Merry could become overly sentimental so he changed the conversation by reaching into his pocket and taking out the wrapped present he had brought her. "Sorry I couldn't get to the wedding, Mercy," he said.

"If there had been any way in the world of finding you, you would have been there, Wayne," she said. "It's the only thing about my wedding and my marriage that I'd change. I had always planned that you'd be at my wedding, you know that."

There was a sincerity in Mercy that made a man feel humble. He thought fleetingly, *You could have found me, Mike,* then said gruffly, "I wanted you to have a little remembrance, anyway." He laid the package on the table.

She was again as eagerly excited as a child. She picked up the package and held it against her breast. "May I open it?"

"If you don't, you'll be a long time wondering what's in it."

She broke the string and tore away the brown paper and tossed aside the tissue underneath. For a moment she stared at the brooch in her hand, and when she looked up there were tears in her eyes. "It's your mother's brooch," she said.

"You're the only other woman I ever found had the same colour hair," Wayne said. There was a sudden mischief in his eyes. "I decided on it the day you asked me to marry you."

"Wayne!" she said, pretending indignation. "I was only six years old. You'll never let me forget it, will you?"

"Why forget that nice a compliment?" he said.

"Oh, Wayne!" She ran forward suddenly and stood on tiptoe and put her arms around his neck and kissed him hard.

"By, golly," he said, "I got to find me a barrel full of those."

She laughed merrily and then seemed no longer able to ignore his split lip and bruised face. Her eyes clouded. He grinned at her and said, "Calf kicked me."

"Oh," she said, embarrassed that he had known her thoughts. Unlike Ruth, she was perfectly willing to let this explanation stand unquestioned.

He spent a pleasant fifteen minutes or so chatting with her, having a cup of coffee, and then he got up to leave. She saw him to the door, reluctant to see him go, he thought. She said finally, "Wayne, is everything all right between you and Mike?"

He glanced at her quickly and glanced away, wondering how much she knew. "Sure," he said. "Everything's fine. Looks like I'll be leasing some grass from him."

"I'm glad, Wayne," she said. "I want you and Mike to be friends."

He took her by the shoulders and shook her gently. "People get old worrying about nothing," he said.

"Then I'll quit worrying," she said. She took his hand. "The brooch is the most wonderful present in the world, Wayne."

"I'm glad you like it, Mercy," he said.

"And you're still the most wonderful man in the world to me."

"Now listen," he said with mock severity. "That kind of talk was all right when you were six years old. You're a big girl now."

She was thoroughly pleased. "Do I embarrass you?"

"If you did." he said, "I'd turn you across my knee, just like I used to do."

"Wayne," she said, "I think you worried more about my growing up than my own father did." She tilted her head, "What did you think would happen to me?"

Not this, he thought. "Why," he said, "I figured you'd do what you said, wait and marry me."

"And I thought you'd marry Ruth, Wayne."

Her directness didn't surprise him at all. He had always treated her as a child. She had always given him a child's confidence. He felt the twinge of old memories and put them aside. "I'm not the marrying kind, Mercy," he said.

"You're not good at lying, either," she said. She stood on tiptoe and kissed his cheek. "But I still love you."

He left her then and went outside. Untying his horse, he swung into the saddle, waving a brief good-bye to Ruth, who had come to stand on the porch at the main house. As he rode away from the ranch, depression claimed him.

He had been backed down. He would have to go to his partners now and admit he had wasted time with his stubbornness. But that in itself seemed of little importance. He kept thinking of Mercy, finding it hard to consider her anything but a child, and he kept thinking of Mike Conaway, knowing Mike was perfectly capable of robbing Anvil and walking out on Mercy. He was capable of it, but would he do it? How could you look inside a man?

You couldn't, Wayne knew. *But I can keep an eye on you, Mike,* Wayne thought. *I can and I will. I can do that much for Ruth and Mercy. And if you ever run out on her, Mike, so help me I'll find you, wherever you are. Some place, sometime, somebody has to put a stake through your spokes. When you married Mercy, you picked me for the job.*

The beauty of broken sun patches on the rain-washed landscape was lost on Wayne as he rode back towards his own ranch.

CHAPTER
5

HAVING NO BUSINESS in town, Wayne took a short-cut trail that saved him a half-hour's riding. He left Anvil range and crossed both Leatherman's and Faull's property, going this way. He had to dismount twice to open barbed-wire gates.

He passed within a few hundred yards of Newton's place, a ranch much like the others, a place of unrealised possibilities. A mowing machine stood in a weed-choked field where it had been left last fall; a wagon, new wheat sprouting from its bed, was pushing against a break in the corral fence. A worthless but likable dog who could do tricks came out to meet Wayne and didn't bother to bark.

He turned up a canyon road and presently came to the protected valley where he had gathered his cattle during the four months he had been back. The shadows crawled thickly into the canyons and spread around the cabin that had been a line shack in the days when the Hardisty ranch had amounted to something. Rows of feeding mangers stood on barren and trampled ground that sloped away from the cabin toward a tiny creek, full now, dry in summer. Roofed-over haystacks were almost completely exhausted. In a fenced pasture along the creek a dozen horses stood in the gathering darkness. They looked up and nickered a greeting as Wayne approached. He glanced over them quickly and saw that his brother Clyde's favourite mount was missing. He wasn't surprised.

He unsaddled his horse and turned him into the fenced pasture. For a moment the animal stood there, spread-legged, shaking the sweat from his hide, then he ran, tail up, starting a miniature stampede among the other horses. Wayne did his few chores before going to the cabin.

The freshness of rain lay heavily over the small valley. Sounds carried, and all around the sharp breaks of the caprock were blue-black against the rapidly clearing sky. A feeling of loneliness spread through the isolated cup in the foothills and a single star came out bright and clean, as if the rain had washed it too. The star blinked out as a laggard cloud scudded across the sky, moved by a wind that was unfelt here below.

Lighting a kerosene lamp, Wayne built up

a fire in the cookstove, more for something to do than anything else, for surprisingly, he wasn't hungry. Perhaps if he waited a while, Clyde would be back. He knew immediately that it was wishful thinking. Clyde wouldn't be back until morning, and then only to pick up his belongings. He knew that after their fight last night, Clyde would have decided to move out. He would go back to the home place, a dilapidated, Virginia-creeper-covered frame house in a grove of locust at the end of the valley. Wayne and Clyde had closed the home place up three months ago in favour of this more convenient location here at the feed lot.

Darkness came swiftly, and in time Wayne gave in to the tiredness that gnawed at him. He opened a can of pork and beans and a can of tomatoes, heated them and ate them without enthusiasm, then undressed and went to bed. He surprised himself by falling asleep immediately.

When he awoke the next morning he glanced first at Clyde's bunk and saw that it was still empty.

With a good night's sleep behind him, he thought guiltily of the fact that he hadn't bothered to tell Leatherman and Faull and

Newton of his capitulation to lease Beaver Creek from Mike Conaway. He half excused himself by saying he wasn't used to having other people dependent on him; actually, he knew he had dreaded the telling. He shrugged it off as unimportant. He'd see them before noon anyway.

He dressed and made himself a quick breakfast of flapjacks, gravy and coffee, then put on a sheepskin-lined coat and went outside into the pre-dawn darkness. The usually hard-packed earth around the cabin had turned to red mud and he had to watch his footing carefully as he went out to the corral. He caught up a horse with no difficulty and, leading the animal over to a lean-to shed, he gave it a bucket of oats, and let it eat while he busied himself similarly feeding a work team. Afterwards he saddled up, mounted, and rode across the empty feed lot past the empty mangers and nearly used-up haystacks and followed a well-defined trail up the creek. He jumped a deer at one of the salt licks he had set out and paid no attention to it as it bounded across his path and into the dripping brush.

The clouds had thickened again during the night and it had started to drizzle. Wayne glanced to the east and saw the breaking dawn and decided that, in spite of the shower, the rain was over.

Topping a low ridge, he came to a sage-brush-choked swale and found what he had been seeking every morning for a week. An old cow bellowed mournfully and at her feet Wayne saw the white-faced calf, no more than a few hours old. There was nothing that scratched the itch in Wayne Hardisty like the sight of a new-born calf. His worry over Mike Conaway and his trouble with Clyde fled his mind. With the smell of wet sage in his nostrils and a new calf on the ground, Wayne Hardisty felt as big as he had once dreamed of being.

He dismounted slowly, keeping an eye on the cow, and he took a good look at the calf— a little bull. Steam curled from the little animal's wet hide. His eyes were as bright as dollars. "How about it, little Money in the Bank?" Wayne said. "Want to come along with me and see the rest of the world?"

The cow bellowed, close to his ear, making a lumbering charge at him. He side-stepped her neatly. "Had to wait until it rained, didn't you, you old rip?" Wayne said to the cow. "Well, you can't stay here unless you want to take the chance of your son being cougar bait." He stooped quickly, getting the calf in his arms, bunching all four feet together. The little animal let out a startled bleat all out of proportion to its size, and the cow, with a frantic bellow, came charging in. Wayne moved swiftly so that his horse was between himself and the cow. "Keep that up and I'll let you have one right between the eyes," he said to the cow.

He manoeuvred his horse around and with a quick movement placed the calf in the saddle, front legs on one side, hind legs on the other. Stepping into the stirrup, he pulled himself up just as the cow made another lunge at him. The calf quit struggling and Wayne grinned down at him. He rode back toward the feed lot, and the mother cow followed along, her head thrust straight out, her protests dull blasts of sound in the thick, wet air.

Back at the cabin, he bedded the calf in fresh straw under the roof of an open shed and forked down some hay from a meagre-stack. The work team had finished with their oats now and he harnessed up and led them to a flat-bed wagon, hitched them, got a pitchfork from the shed and drove the wagon to the nearest haystack.

Wayne worked steadily, filling the mangers, until almost ten, glancing toward the cabin often, expecting Clyde. He was coming in, ready to put up the team, when he saw the two riders approaching the cabin. A quick tension ran through him and he stepped down from the wagon and carefully wrapped the lines around the brake. It was Rudy Effinger, the butcher, and his partner, Lorry Calvin. Wayne walked across the barnyard and was standing in front of the cabin when Effinger and Calvin reined up. Wayne looked at Effinger and said, "So you brought your bogeyman with you, did you, Rudy?"

Calvin folded his hands on the saddle horn and appraised the corral and gathering cattle as casually as a neighbour who had dropped by to pass the time of day.

"I got a paper here," Rudy Effinger said. "For six beeves. If you're busy, Lorry and me will cut out six and give you a look at 'em. There don't need to be any trouble about it."

"There don't need to be, maybe," Wayne said, "but there will be if you try it. You want to turn around and head back, or you want to start it now?"

Lorry Calvin turned his slow gaze on Wayne. He dismounted then with an ease and gracefulness that said plainly that he hadn't always worked in a slaughterhouse. Every movement he made had that same liquid flow, a perfect co-ordination of muscle and mind. Lorry gave his horse a sudden slap and the animal bolted with a grunt of surprise, ran a few feet, then trotted over to the corral fence. In that simple movement Lorry Calvin had left himself standing there alone, facing Wayne Hardisty. He had said plainly that he had intention of running or backing down. Oddly enough, he spoke to Rudy, not to Wayne. "You've made your brag, Rudy," Lorry said. "Now back it up."

There was momentary surprise in Rudy Effinger's eyes and then he too dismounted. Neither Lorry nor Effinger was armed and Wayne thought, *Either you knew Clyde wasn't here or somebody in this crowd figures he's pretty big, and it's not you, Rudy.* Effinger took two steps forward and stopped stolidly, his short, stocky legs spread. "I'm gonna get what's coming to me, Hardisty," he said.

"Damned if I don't believe you are, Rudy," Wayne said.

Rudy spoke across his shoulder. "Go cut out six steers, Lorry. Two-year-olds ought to do it."

Calvin was watching this with amused curiosity. "Not yet," he said.

"Then I will," Rudy said. He turned abruptly and put his foot in the stirrup and Wayne moved in on him. He caught Rudy by the coat and jerked him away from the horse.

"You'll whip me first, Rudy," Wayne said quietly.

There was no further escape now and Rudy knew it. He shot a swift glance at Lorry and saw Lorry walking away, over toward the corral fence. He saw Lorry stop at the fence and lean there, intent on watching the horses. There was a moment of panic in Rudy Effinger as he realised he had to hold up his end of this. He said. "You've shoved me once too often, Hardisty," and he threw himself forward, half turned, his left shoulder down.

Rudy's shoulder collided solidly with Wayne's chest and as it did Rudy twisted, putting the entire strength of his shoulders into the short drive of his right fist. He knew right then he had made a mistake. He had aimed for Wayne's short ribs, but Wayne, anticipating the blow, had turned with it and Rudy felt his savage power wasted on Wayne's sheepskin-lined coat.

Rudy tried to recover his balance. He was half turned, his thick, squat body settled in a crouch, his jaw fully exposed, when Wayne hit him.

Sitting on the top rail of the corral fence now, Lorry Calvin watched with studious interest.

Rudy felt the impact of that blow but he had presence of mind enough to close in and throw his arms around Wayne's body. He locked his fingers and threw his strength into the embrace, hanging on. Wayne dug the power of his legs against the slimy mud and they both fell and Rudy was on the bottom, his bear hug broken.

Wayne clawed his way over Rudy's threshing legs and got his knees on Rudy's shoulders and then the full savageness of his anger hit him and he started driving great, looping blows into Rudy's face. Several times Rudy managed to free himself by kicking his feet and literally bucking free, but each time Wayne rolled on him, pinned his shoulders and smashed his face again.

Both men were slimed with mud now. Rudy got his shoulders free, sat up and tried to lock his arms around Wayne again, butting Wayne in the face with his head. Wayne got a handful of Effinger's hair and yanked the butcher's head back and kept yanking it until Effinger's grip around his body slipped or broke. They rolled and again Wayne was on top, and now he knew he had won and he drove his fist against Effinger's exposed jaw, wanting to end it. He had forgotten Lorry Calvin completely. He didn't remember until he felt the paralysing impact of Calvin's boot toe against his ribs.

"That's enough, Hardisty," Lorry Calvin said. "You've whipped him. Now try me."

Wayne got to his feet, gasping for breath. His legs felt rubbery and his eyes were blurred. He reached up to wipe mud from his face and as he did, Calvin hit him.

The blow was sharp, accurate. It landed almost exactly between Wayne's eyes. A thousand lights exploded and Wayne staggered backward, fighting now to keep his footing, and he collided sharply with the wall of the shed.

The impact seemed to clear his brain some. He shook his head and saw Calvin coming toward him. Calvin had a six-shooter in his right hand.

Wayne looked at Calvin and believed he had never seen such supreme confidence in his life. Calvin had had a gun in his saddle bag, apparently. He had wandered over to the corral and got his gun during the fight, preparing for this moment, knowing it would arrive. Wayne felt the wall of the shed against his back. He said, "I got a shotgun in the cabin, Calvin. Let me go get it and I'll accommodate you."

Calvin shook his head. "I don't trust guns," he said. "They go off sometimes."

A voice from the corner of the cabin said "They do at that, Calvin. Drop yours."

Wayne's gaze jerked to the corner of the cabin. His brother Clyde, mounted, was there. Clyde had his saddle carbine in his hand, pointed directly at Lorry Calvin's back. There was a crisp sound of well-fitting mechanism as Clyde levered a shell into the carbine. "Drop it, Calvin," he said.

That frozen grin was still on Lorry Calvin's face, an ugly thing that looked almost as if the man's facial muscles had once been paralysed and were no longer functioning properly. He said, "You want to make this a party, little brother?"

"I'll make it a funeral if you don't drop that gun," Clyde Hardisty said.

Calvin shrugged his shoulders. "There's always another time," he said. His fingers opened and the gun dropped into the mud. He glanced down at it as if he were more concerned about the welfare of the gun than he was his own.

Wayne moved away from the shed wall. "Speaking of parties, Calvin," he said, "I think this is our dance."

"Stop it, Wayne," Clyde said.

Wayne paused and looked up at his younger brother. "Why?"

"Because it's not your fight," Clyde said. "It's mine. I told you to stay out of it; I'm telling you again. If you had kept out of it in the first place it wouldn't have gone this far. Now, damned if I'll be responsible for you getting yourself killed."

Rudy Effinger was heaving himself out of the mud. He paused a moment on hands and knees and then staggered to his feet. He was an ugly sight, his face blood smeared, his clothes slicked to his body with the red mud. Wayne saw the decision in Clyde's eyes, the steadiness of the rifle. "What, then?" Wayne said.

"There's a law against pulling a gun on a man," Clyde said. "Against trespassing, too. I'll see to it they both get time to think about it." He looked directly at Wayne and said, "You trust me to take care of it, or do you want to come along and make sure I wipe my nose right?"

Wayne looked at his brother, a handsome, well-built man four years younger than himself. He said stubbornly, "I'll go along," and immediately wondered why he hadn't admitted he was going to town anyway? What in the devil was the matter with him that he deliberately antagonized Clyde this way? He walked stiffly toward the corral and caught up a horse, then made one concession. "They're your playmates," he said to Clyde "You got the gun. You herd 'em. I'll go along for the ride."

The marks of last night's fight were clearly visible on Clyde's handsome face. There was a hard frostiness in his eyes and something that was near disgust in his expression. He said, "It would kill you to see somebody do something on their own, wouldn't it?"

By the time Clyde had delivered his two prisoners to Don Lien, the marshal, sworn out a complaint against them and seen them lodged safely in jail, the news was all over town. Lee Leatherman and Bob Faull found Wayne at the Emporium rigging himself out in new clothes to replace the mud-ruined outfit he had worn. The sincere concern of his partners and their willingness to help made Wayne ashamed that he hadn't gone to them last night.

"Lorry and Rudy will get thirty days unless somebody bails them out," Wayne said, "and I don't know, anybody who would. They'll cool off some by that time."

"I always knew Calvin would reach for a gun in a pinch," Lee Leatherman said. "I don't like it, Wayne."

Wayne chuckled. "I like it less, Lee, I'm the one had the gun in my belly." He looked at a blue hickory shirt and tossed it aside. "Newton come in with you?"

"Not with us," Lee said, "but I see his rig in town."

"Get hold of him while I change clothes," Wayne said. "I saw Mike Conaway when I rode in. We might as well sign that lease with him."

He saw a quick relief in Lee's and Bob's eyes, but they made no comment and he respected them for that. He was backing down, admitting he had been stubborn because of a personal grudge, but these men weren't going to gloat about it. He wanted to clear up the matter entirely then and he said, "I talked to Brod. Like you boys figured, he wouldn't back down. We deal with Mike or we don't deal."

He closed the matter there and as he watched Faull and Leatherman leave the store he thought with some amusement, *That wasn't hard. Could it be I'm beginning to realize there's somebody in the world besides Wayne Hardisty?* He nodded to the clerk and said, "I'll take these, Roy. Put 'em on my bill if I've still got credit."

"Your credit's all right, Wayne," the merchant said. "I couldn't help overhearing you say you got some grass."

"It makes a difference, don't it?" Wayne said.

The merchant grinned sheepishly. "Well, I don't suspect that Montana drover would be much interested in starting out with cows that hadn't eaten in two months, would he?"

"He wouldn't," Wayne said. "Can I change there in the back room?"

"Sure," Roy said. "Anything else you need?"

Wayne scooped up the bundle of clothes and started to move away from the counter, then hesitated. He half-turned and said, "Yeah, maybe there is. Pick me out a .44 Colt's six-shooter and some shells for it, will you? The weather will be warming up soon and the snakes will be getting thick."

The merchant felt a dryness in his mouth and he ran his tongue across his lips. "Sure,

Wayne," he said. "Sure, I'll pick you out one."

Don Lien, the town marshal, sauntered away from the jail and across to the hotel and found Mike Conaway at the hotel's bar. He moved up alongside Mike and signalled the bar-tender for his noon drink. The marshal was a leathery little old man with weary blue eyes and a long, drooping moustache. He had been here a long time and he had seen them come and go and he didn't care a lot about any of them. He took his drink, two thirds water, one third whiskey, and tested it with his lips. He said then, "Couple of customers of mine want to see you, Mike." He looked into the back bar mirror, not at Mike Conaway.

Mike nearly choked on his drink. "Effinger and Calvin?"

"Those two," the marshal said.

"What the devil about?"

"I wouldn't know," the marshal said. "I didn't ask."

"Well, they can go to the devil," Mike Conaway said. "I don't want anything to do with those two."

The marshal shrugged his thin shoulders. "It's your privilege," he said. "They asked me to tell you. I told you." He finished his drink with one gulp and went outside, giving his noon glance to the clearing weather.

Mike poured himself another drink. A moment before he had been standing here supremely contented with himself. He had had a long talk with Ruth last night and he knew that Ruth had about reached the end of her rope with Clyde. It had been slow, delicate business, this thing of breaking up the engagement between Ruth and Clyde. This had seemed all important to Mike once, for he had thought first of staying here. Now he only thought to himself, *Go ahead and get married. I won't be at the wedding. . . .*

His thoughts turned swiftly to Wayne Hardisty and then to Brod Manwaring. He knew Wayne had been out to see Brod; he knew Brod had refused to deal with Wayne on Beaver Creek. Mike now had Wayne where he wanted him. When Wayne saw the terms of the Beaver Creek lease Mike had drawn up, Mike was positive Wayne would refuse to sign. A split-up between Wayne and his partners would logically follow, for Mike had already indicated to Leatherman, Faull and Newton that they might be able to get a much better deal if Wayne's personal and unreasonable antagonism were out of the picture. Mike hadn't come out and said so, but the implication was there. And with Wayne out of the way, there was nothing to keep Mike Conaway from heading for Montana with a herd of Anvil cows. And when he received payment for that herd, there was nothing to make him come back here with the money.

He glanced around now and saw that he was the only one at the bar and his curiosity came back to what the marshal had just said. Mike had spoken the truth when he had told the marshal he wanted nothing to do with Rudy Effinger and Lorry Calvin. On the other hand, he knew he couldn't afford to antagonize them too much. It would be a nasty business if the truth about that poker game and Mike's offer to sell a few cows to Effinger got back to Brod right at this time. *The devil with it,* he thought. *A couple of Anvil steers will shut them up. It can't hurt to talk to them.* He paid for his drink and went out on to the street.

Glancing toward the Emporium he saw Wayne Hardisty come through the door and stand there for a moment. Not knowing why he did it, Mike moved down his own side of the street and cut across at the corner rather than angling across where he would have had to meet Wayne. He went into the marshal's office and found Don Lien tilted back in a swivel chair, his hands laced across his lean middle. Lien opened one eye and said, "You won't have trouble findin' 'em. They're the only ones in there."

"I don't know what the devil they want with me," Mike said.

"Ask 'em," the marshal said.

Mike walked down the corridor, through a barred door that was standing open and came to the block of four cells. He glanced in and saw Rudy Effinger stretched out on a bunk. Calvin was leaning tiredly against the cell door, whistling a senseless tune between his wide-spread front teeth. With his lips pulled tight, and the heavy crow's feet at the corners of his eyes, his face looked like a death mask. He stopped whistling momentarily and said, "Bail us out, Conaway."

Startled, Mike said, "What?"

"You heard me," Calvin said. "You're the big man in this country. You can do it. Bail us out."

Mike said warily, "Why should I?"

Calvin turned slowly. He gripped the bars with his hands and looked steadily at Mike

Conaway. There was something about Calvin's gaze that made it impossible to turn away from the man. There was no anger in it, no threat. There was just that exasperating confidence. "You got things nice, Conaway," Lorry said. "A pretty wife, a big ranch about to drop into your hands. You want to keep it that way, don't you?"

"Listen, Lorry," Mike said hotly. "If you think you can buffalo me just because I set in a card game with you—"

"You didn't just set in," Lorry said. "You helped me run the cards."

"What about it?" Mike said. "It's my word against yours. And you're in jail."

"Come on, Mike," Calvin said pleasantly. "Bail us out."

"You can rot in here for all I care."

"But we won't, Mike," Lorry Calvin said. "Thirty days is the most we can get. Then we get out."

"So you get out."

Lorry shrugged his shoulders as if he had given up the whole idea. And suddenly his eyes were on Mike again, amused, colourless, confident, his smile wide. He said, "I hear tell Wayne Hardisty went out to see Brod Manwaring about getting a better deal on that Beaver Creek lease."

"Suppose he did?" Mike said. "What's that to you?"

"Nothing," Lorry said. "Just give me an idea, that's all." He was laughing now. There was no sound, but he was laughing. "You're hard to deal with, Mike," he said. "I reckon when me and Rudy get out we ought to do the same as Wayne did. We'll go out and see Brod and see if we can't get a better deal on that beef you offered to sell us."

The threat was plain. Lorry wouldn't hesitate a minute to go to Brod and tell the old man that Mike was selling a few Anvil cows on the side. *Try it,* Mike thought. *Your word against mine.*

Rudy Effinger groaned and rolled over. For the first time Mike saw his face, swollen, shapeless, his lips mangled, his eyes nearly closed. *Wayne did that,* Mike thought swiftly, and he knew the crawling in his stomach was fear. He thought of Wayne and Brod and that unexplainable closeness he knew was between them. If Lorry were to accuse Mike of stealing beef, Brod might ask Wayne about it. *And Brod might take Wayne's word over mine.* Mike saw Lorry's expressionless eyes searching his face, saw that knowing grin. . . . "Hell with you!" Mike said explosively. He turned and walked rapidly down the corridor.

Don Lien wasn't in the office and Mike walked on through, out on to the street. The sun was out bright and it slapped against him like a searchlight. He stood there a moment, feeling as if every eye in town were on him, then he hurried on up the street.

Damn Wayne Hardisty, he thought savagely. *You'll keep riding me, won't you? Why? What did I ever do to you? What's it to you if I had another woman before Mercy? Is that a crime? I married Mercy, didn't I? She's my wife. . . .*

Wife. A sudden weariness hit him. It was hard to think of Mercy as his wife. Even the half-breed girl had had more sense than Mercy. At least the half-breed girl had fight in her. . . . Perspiration glued Mike's shirt to his back. Damn that affair anyway. He hadn't meant to kill the girl. He had only meant to frighten her. But when he told her he was leaving she came at him like a tiger, screaming at him that she was going to have a baby, that he couldn't leave her, that he had to marry her. . . .

Forget that, he thought. *It's over. There's no charge against you. There never has been. Not even suspicion. . . .* Again he knew he was wrong. There was suspicion. In Wayne Hardisty's mind. But what difference did it make? What could Wayne Hardisty do with unfounded suspicion? Go to Mercy? Mike laughed inwardly. *Try it, Hardisty. I've covered that. She already knows and there's one place your word won't be any good over mine. Not with Mercy.*

And Mike had told her—told her his own way, just as the authorities had it on the records. Mercy had held Mike's head in her lap and cried softly. She had stroked Mike's hair and whispered over and over, "Poor Mike. My poor, poor Mike. It's a bad dream, darling. It's over and gone. My poor Mike. . . . *I convinced her,* he thought. *So quit riding me, Hardisty. Leave me alone. It won't do you any good.*

Mike wanted a drink. He turned into the bar at the hotel and saw Don Lien standing there, talking idly with Wayne Hardisty. He saw Wayne glance at him, saw that knowing expression in Wayne's eyes, the expression that said as plainly as print, *I know you, Mike. I know you can't play it straight. You'll try to get away with something, and when you do, I'll be here to see it. . . .* Wayne's quiet voice jarred him as hard as if Wayne had reached out and touched him.

"Leatherman and Faull and Newton will be along in a minute," Wayne said. "You drive a hard bargain, Mike."

"No harder than Brod would drive, is it?" Mike said. He felt a small glow of triumph that was hard to conceal.

"Too hard to let a man make a living," Wayne said. He didn't seem angry. Maybe he was even glad. Now he could drift on, just as he had been drifting the first time Mike met him. *You're a lot like me,* Mike thought. *You can only stay in one place so long and then it gets to pressing in on you.*

"No hard feelings?" Mike said.

"None at all," Wayne said. "It's just business. Have a drink on it?"

And for a moment there, some of the old companionship was back between them and then Mike thought, *He's giving up. It's going my way.* He laughed at something Wayne said. "We had some good times, Wayne," Mike said. "Real good times. Moving around scratches an itch in a man, no doubt about it. But once you find the right woman—settle down. . . ."

"You're real settled, huh, Mike?" Wayne said lazily.

"Real settled, Wayne."

"That's good," Wayne said. He threw a

fifty-cent piece on the bar. "See you in a little while," he said.

Mike stood there, watching Wayne's broad back disappear through the door. He thought of a herd of three thousand cattle, delivered in Montana and immediately turned the amount into money. *Real good times,* he thought. *But I'll have better ones. Ninety thousand dollars worth. . . .*

It was going good. He couldn't let anything spoil it now. Not anything. He thought of Lorry Calvin. Suppose he did go bail for Lorry and Effinger? He could explain his way out of that a lot easier than he could explain the fact that he had offered to sell them beef behind Brod's back. He turned to Don Lien and said casually, "What would it cost to bail Effinger and Calvin out?"

There was no surprise in the marshal's eyes. There was no expression whatsoever. This was business. It was a business question. "Five hundred ought to do it," he said.

"Have to be cash?"

"Not for you, I reckon," the marshal said.

"All right," Mike said. "I'll go it. Leave 'em in for three or four days to cool off. I'd rather have those two for friends than enemies."

"Most folks would," the marshal said

tonelessly. "I guess Hardisty don't care." There was nothing you could read in his voice. "You'll have to sign a paper," the marshal said. "There ain't much to it."

CHAPTER
6

LEE LEATHERMAN, BOB FAULL and Bennett Newton got a bottle no one of them could rightly afford and sat down at a table in the hotel bar for a few minutes of the most complete relaxation they had known in four months. Along with Wayne Hardisty, they had just put their names to Mike Conaway's lease on the lush Beaver Creek range and their worry over how they would hold their pool herd of a thousand cattle for the next two months was over and done with.

The lease was ridiculously exorbitant, but it had been a friendly enough meeting and Wayne had carried off his end of it with unusual graciousness. He had even had a drink with Mike to seal the bargain and the two of them had momentarily reminisced of other days and other places when they had ridden together over most of Wyoming, Colorado and Montana.

Speaking of that now, Leatherman savoured his drink with the enjoyment of a man who hadn't tasted good whiskey for a long time. He shook his head. "Wayne's a hard one to figure," he said. "He'd argue about his own name, and then he turns right around and takes anything Brod Manwaring says as gospel." He glanced at his partners, a hint of the old worry in his eyes. "You think there's any chance Mike will soften up on the prices? He hinted he might."

"He won't," Bob Faull said promptly. "We signed a lease. He'll hold us to it. As long as Wayne's in it, anyway. I'd a signed with Mike two months ago if it hadn't been for Wayne. You all know that. I'd a signed as soon as we found out we wasn't gonna get that grass we thought we had lined up."

"We'll break even and little more," Newton said.

"It's better than losin' it all, ain't it?" Faull said. "Without Beaver Creek, that's what we'd do."

"One thing," Leatherman said philosophically, "we won't be any worse off than we were when we went into this with Wayne.

"Wayne makes a proposition sound good," Faull said.

"There's a streak of his dad in him, I

88

reckon," Newton said. "His dad always had some big deal on his mind that sounded fine, but once you got into it and took a close look at it, it was as full of holes as a cow with screw worms."

Leatherman sipped his drink thoughtfully. "What kind of a man do you suppose Mike Conaway really is?" he said.

"I sorta feel sorry for Mike," Newton said. "Notice how nervous he was around us today? He knows darned well everybody is talkin' about how he married himself a good thing."

"From what I've seen of Mike, Mercy Manwaring could have done a lot worse," Bob Faull said.

"Thinkin' of Clyde and Ruth?" Leatherman suggested idly.

"I don't figure that's none of our business, Lee," Bob Faull said. "We're in this thing four ways. Us three here, Clyde and Wayne together. How Clyde and Wayne handle their quarter of it is their affair, not ours."

"And that's the way I'm willing to leave it," Leatherman said. "But when you get a couple like Effinger and Calvin mixed up in it . . ."

"You know what it was about, don't you?" Newton asked.

Faull shrugged. "A poker debt Clyde owed, wasn't it?"

"That's part of it," Newton said. He glanced around the room, then half closed his eyes and a knowing smile lifted one corner of his mouth. The whiskey was warm in his stomach; he felt important. "It started over Ruth Manwaring," Newton said, speaking without moving his lips. "Guess the fire wasn't plumb out between her and Wayne, and Clyde found out about it. Clyde and Wayne fought it out; then when it came to Clyde payin' off his poker debt with beef, Wayne got stubborn and wouldn't back it up."

"Where'd yuh hear that?" Leatherman demanded.

"Hell," Newton said, "it's all over town."

"Wayne can be damned bull-headed," Faull said. "It ain't like him to welch on a bet, though."

"Ain't you never heard about it being all fair in love and war?" Newton said with his mysterious smile.

"I get a little tired of Wayne thinkin' everything's got to go his way or no way," Faull said.

Newton made fists of his hands and laid them both on the table. He stared at them a long time then looked up suddenly. "Why don't we say what we're thinkin', boys?"

An embarrassment ran between the three men.

"I wouldn't cut Wayne out," Leatherman said. "This was his idea in the first place. You got to give him credit for that."

"We'd be better off with him out of it," Faull said.

There was a visible relief around the table now that this was out in the open. "We might as well face it," Newton said. "The terms on that lease with Mike was a direct slap against Wayne, not against us three, and damned if I blame Mike for it, the way Wayne's been ridin' him. Mike would have come more than halfway if Wayne would have given him a chance."

There was a deep silence between them as they considered the seriousness of what they were saying. It was Leatherman who made the decision. "Wayne's the one signed the contract to supply a thousand stockers to his Montana friend," Lee said. "Without Wayne there wouldn't have been no contract, and without Wayne and Clyde now we'd be short two hundred fifty, three hundred head. We went into this together. I figger we better see it through that way." He looked around the table. "You asked me. That's my say."

The others nodded quick agreement. Newton said, "It was on our minds. I figgered it would be best if we come out and laid it on the table." He leaned back in his chair. The whiskey was building a satisfied contentment and sense of well-being in him. "Next year's another time," he said.

"It is," Leatherman said. "We've all learned a lot in the last four months. We deliver a herd of prime stockers this year and other outfits back in Montana are gonna hear about it. The price will go up and so will the demand. I figure we can get backing to raise a herd of five thousand next year." He downed his drink quickly. "We won't have to be piddlin' around with two, three hundred cows apiece, boys. We can pool with Anvil if we want to."

Faull and Newton had obviously considered the same thing. Newton said, "I don't know as I want to be the one tells Wayne he can't come in with us next year."

"I wouldn't worry about it," Leatherman said. "If Wayne ain't here, we won't have to tell him."

Faull looked up quickly. "What'cha mean by that?"

"I'll bet yuh a hundred he won't be here, that's all," Leatherman said.

"You think he'll drift again?" Newton asked.

"Think of it," Leatherman said. "What's to hold him?" He sipped his whiskey and sighed deeply. "When a man starts lookin' for the other side of the mountain he sees another mountain. You think Wayne's just bein' stubborn?" Lee shook his head. "He's restless, that's all. When that trail herd heads for Montana, Wayne'll go with it, and damned if I blame him. If I didn't have a wife and six kids, I'd go with it myself."

"It would be nice at that, wouldn't it?" Faull said softly. "Sleepin' out under the stars—seein' new country every day—gettin' paid for somethin' you really enjoyed doin' . . ." He shook his head. "A young man gets to thinkin' there ain't nothin' he wants more in the world than a family and a little place of his own. He never stops to figger what he's givin' up, does he?"

"It's the trouble with the world," Newton said. "A man never gets a chance to do what he really wants to do." He became confidential. "You know what I always wanted to do?" He waited dramatically. "Work on a river boat on the Columbia," he said.

Faull and Leatherman thought that over with great seriousness. "I can see how a man might want that," Faull said finally. "Me now, it wouldn't suit." He cocked one eye. "Recollect that whiskey drummer that come through here few months back? Had good clothes, didn't he? Bought a drink for everybody in the house three times around, didn't he?" He downed his drink, slammed the shot glass down, then sighed and shook his head, thinking of opportunity lost. "I would have stepped right into a job," Faull said. "Travel all over Oregon and Washington and Idaho—"

"Sellin' whiskey?" Leatherman asked.

"Why not?" Faull said. "I give this drummer a couple of ideas I had. He said, 'How come you to have merchandizing ideas like that?' I reckon he figgered he'd back me down, puttin' it to me that way. I looked him right in the eye and I said, 'I don't reckon you ever read Miekel's *Theory of Applied Salesmanship*, did you?' Well, you ought to seen it hit him."

Leatherman shook his head and laughed softly. "Son of a gun. Tied him right up, did yuh, Bob?"

"You know," Newton said, "the three of us ought to set down like this more often.

Hell, here we are partners and we don't even know each other."

"A man lets the worthwhile things get away from him," Leatherman said. "For instance, take books. How long's it been since you two set down and talked about books?"

"I played it cagey," Bob Faull said. "I seen this drummer knowed I'd outfoxed him, throwin' Miekel's *Theory* at him that way. He said to me, 'Say I'd like to talk to you. It ain't often I find a man well versed on salesmanship.'"

"Been ten years since I read a book," Leatherman said. "Poetry, by John, there's a thing. Poetry. 'It was the schooner Hesperus and she sailed the wintry sea and the Cap'n taken his little daughter to keep him company.' Doggies, there was a good 'un!"

"I said, 'Maybe I might be interested and maybe I might not be,'" Faull went on. "'A man's got to look at the gross business present and lay it against the gross business potential to arrive at his possible commission earned,' I said to him." Faull chuckled, remembering. "Hell, you could a knocked his eyes off with a stick, way they was buggin' out. He says to me, 'Say, now, you stay away from my boss, you hear? First thing you know you'd be sales manager and I'd be workin' for you."

"That's the big trouble with folks today," Newton said. "They never take the time to get to know each other."

Leatherman said, "Wasn't there one went, 'And I don't want no moanin' when I walk into the bar'? Feller worked for my daddy once used to say it. It was a dandy."

"There was the job," Faull said, talking to himself now. "Sales manager. But I'd a had to move to Portland, pull up roots. It ain't fair to the wife and kids, the way I figger. A man's married, he's got responsibilities."

"That's why I never got married," Wayne Hardisty said. He had come in while they were talking and he had stood there a moment, unnoticed. All three men got up and made a commotion of getting a fourth chair, making room for him at the table.

"By golly, we wondered where you was," Faull said. "Thought we ought to have a couple of cheers together. The three of us went in on the bottle."

"Ain't my money good?" Wayne said. He grinned. "I got my neck just as far into Mike Conaway's noose as you boys. Here, I'll go my share." He took a fifty-cent piece from his pocket and tossed it on the table. "Now that I bought in, how about lettin' me taste it?"

The bar-tender brought over another glass and the bottle passed solemnly around the table as each man poured his own drink. Leatherman raised his glass with the dignity of a Viking at a wedding feast. "We ought to toast to it," he said.

"To Montana," Wayne said, raising his glass.

"That's good," Leatherman said. "To Montana.

There was a long silence between them and finally Newton said, "What's it like, Wayne?"

"Montana?" Wayne said. He poured himself another drink and tilted back in his chair. Holding the drink in his hand, he stared into its amber depths with a quizzical smile on his lips. "It ain't a place really," he said. "It's more like a state of mind. If you want to know what it looks like, it depends on what part you're lookin' at. Mostly it's high and wide. Bigger than all get out. You cross the mountains and they sort of keep nudgin' you on, and there's the old Missouri invitin' you to come down to New Orleans. You know you ain't goin', but there's a kinda blue haze in the air that throws you out of step with yourself and you ain't sure but what maybe you will go. You get a sort of homesick feelin' all the time, but you ain't homesick for home. It's for something that's out there yonder. You don't know where, and you really don't much give a damn." He stopped suddenly, the grin on his face boyish and wide. He downed his drink. "Montana's pretty," he said.

His partners glanced at each other knowingly. "To Montana, then," Lee Leatherman said.

Leaving the hotel later, Wayne felt the strike of the afternoon sun after the darkness of the bar room and mused as he had on other occasions that the sunlight always looked different to a man when he had had a few drinks in the middle of the afternoon.

A conservative drinker, Wayne felt the whiskey more than he cared to admit, its effects manifesting themselves mostly in a sense of well-being such as he hadn't felt since his return to Three Rivers after his father's death. It was a good feeling, not unlike the feeling a man had when he was on his own with an unknown trail ahead and a good horse to carry him over it.

The lease they had just signed, as ridiculous as it was in its demands, seemed relatively unimportant. He had at least had the satisfaction of letting Mike know he, Wayne, knew what he was signing. Wayne hated above all else to be taken for a fool. He had signed the lease with Mike standing near his elbow and he had seen Mike's nervousness and anxiety and known it for what it was. For a moment he had nearly felt sorry for Mike. Maybe a man could change, and if he could, a girl like Mercy would be the one to change him. *Maybe I've got you all wrong, Mike.* Then he thought of the Mike he had known. The Mike who had always played a woman for what he could get, the Mike who had said a hundred times that someday he'd really find a soft touch. And he thought of one of Mike's many conquests, murdered. . . .

Stop it, he thought *It's the whiskey.* Actually, the whiskey had been no more than a trigger release to an accumulating and mounting tension that had to give in some direction.

He went up to the stable and visited pleasantly with Pete for a while, talking mostly about his father, Brod's sickness, the excellent range conditions, easily avoiding any mention of Clyde or his run-in with Effinger and Calvin. He mounted his horse then and rode back toward town and the mood of well-being stayed with him until he tied his horse to the rail in front of the Emporium and went in to pick up the gun he had ordered.

With the weight of the gun in his hand, he was unable to ignore its significance. He hadn't misjudged Lorry Calvin. He knew he wasn't through with the man. And suddenly the entire dirty business of Mike Conaway's marriage to Mercy Manwaring was back on him again like an oppressive cloud. An eventual fight with Lorry Calvin was a thing a man could take in his hand and examine, just as he was now examining his gun. But the business of Mike Conaway was a worrisome intangible that was always there, as big and as real as a wall in a man's face, yet always a wall that was invisible to those most concerned. Again he thought, *Why don't I leave it alone?* and again he knew he couldn't. This was the stand he had to take—the stand he had never taken before. This was the point in life where a man met himself face to face and learned to live with himself.

The clerk said, "Do you want a belt and holster for that, Wayne?"

Wayne was jerked abruptly back to the present. "No need," he said. "I didn't figure on wearing it for looks."

CHAPTER
7

THE DAYS WERE growing noticeably longer, Wayne thought, as he rode back toward his own place. He cut across the lower end of the Beaver Creek range, knowing it so thoroughly that he could judge the condition of grass in other parts of the nearly two sections of land with fair accuracy by looking at this, the lower end of it. Beaver Creek, to Wayne, was as beautiful as any range he had ever seen anywhere. He had roamed every inch of its many canyons as a boy; he had lazed the length of the narrow valley, taking trout from the creek that gave the section its name. Every pleasant memory of childhood was directly tied in with Beaver Creek. When his father, borrowing heavily, had lost this range to Brod Manwaring, it was as if Wayne's one tie with home had been cut. The one chance he had seen to make a go of the cattle business had been knocked out from under him, and he hadn't even had a say in it. It wasn't until Beaver Creek was lost that Wayne knew the amount of money his father had borrowed from Brod Manwaring.

In the driest summers, Beaver Creek valley produced a fine stand of meadow hay, and during the spring months, the slopes of each of the numerous side canyons raised grass enough to support a good portion of the pool herd into the first of summer. With this grass and what grass each of the partners had of their own, there wouldn't be any trouble pulling a thousand head through until delivery time. They would be overstocking the range and Wayne knew it, but it was the only solution. It would be a start, and next year was another time.

He rode on, plans building in his mind, and when he came to his cabin he saw Clyde's saddler and a loaded pack horse standing there. Wayne went to the barn and unsaddled and turned out his horse before going to the cabin, reluctant to face an unpleasant situation, unable to avoid it. He went inside and sat down in a chair and watched Clyde, a scowl on his face, sorting through some inconsequential odds and ends.

There was an undeniable handsomeness

about Clyde. His face was clean-shaven, naturally dark, for he resembled his mother's side of the family. His hair was black and tightly curly, neatly groomed. His nose was thin, his eyes brown and serious. The mellow afternoon sun, slanting through the cabin window, accented the bruises on Clyde's left cheek and on his forehead. He was a well-built man, as tall as Wayne, four years younger. He stopped his aimless searching finally, turned and the two brothers regarded each other with hostile self-consciousness. Wayne pushed his hat back off his forehead. "We signed the lease with Mike," Wayne said. "It seems maybe you should have been in on it."

"I said I was dropping out, didn't I?" Clyde said.

"A man can change his mind."

"I haven't."

"You leaving, then?"

"Did you think I wouldn't?"

"No," Wayne said. "I expected you would. You decided on what you want to do?"

"Most anything," Clyde said. "So long as it's not with you."

"I was thinking of the herd and the land. Poor as it is, we still own four hundred acres of rocks and juniper. There's another hundred and eighty of damn good bottom land there at the old home place."

"I'll take the home place," Clyde said. "You take the foothill range and all the cattle."

"You've put in as much work as I have with these cows," Wayne said. "You've got an even split coming."

The anger was hard and brittle in Clyde Hardisty's eyes. "That's it," he said. "See that little brother gets a fair split. He's not big enough to make his own decision."

"What's fair is fair," Wayne said.

"You're noble, Wayne," Clyde said. "You're just as noble as hell."

Wayne expelled a gusty sigh. He settled back in his chair, trying to remember the anger that had led him and Clyde into a fist fight, finding it as impossible to recall anger as it was to recall pain. Once emotions were gone, they were gone. He should know that by now, he guessed, and was immediately thinking of Ruth. He channelled his thoughts of her by saying, "Did Ruth tell you I talked to Brod?"

"Should she have?"

"I figured Brod would ease up a little on the lease terms." He was trying his best to be objective.

"Was that it?" Clyde said. His temper was close to the surface.

"What else?"

"I thought maybe you went out to tell him what a hell of a mistake his daughters made picking the men they did."

Wayne's anger came quickly. "I thought of it," he said.

"You should have told him," Clyde said. "It would have been the noble thing to do." He turned and faced Wayne fully and the bruises were plain on his face. "Come on out in the open, Wayne," he said. "I know what you're up to."

"Then tell me."

"You make me sick," Clyde said. "You and your holier-than-thou game. You think there's still a chance, do you? You think maybe you can make Ruth see what a fine, noble man she missed?"

"Shut up, Clyde."

Clyde moved across the room, directly toward Wayne. He gripped the edge of the table until his knuckles were white, and he leaned forward. "You're so damn noble you stink," he said. "And the only thing you've got against Mike Conaway is that Mike happened to marry a girl with money. You think I haven't talked to Mike? You think he hasn't told me how you had it all figured out that a little waiting would make Ruth come to you?"

"You through?"

"No," Clyde Hardisty said, and now his voice was quiet. "Not until I tell you I hate your guts. Not until I tell you that coppering your bets by taking care of little brother won't do you a damn bit of good. You think Mike Conaway drives a hard bargain? Come around and see me when I've got something to say about leasing Anvil graze, and when you come, make damn sure you come crawling on your belly."

Wayne stood up slowly. The original anger was in him again, growing and pushing against him. He started to reach across the table and then checked himself. He closed his hand into a fist and withdrew it. "All right," he said. "If that's the way you've got it figured."

"That's the way I've got it figured," Clyde Hardisty said. "Just be careful that halo you're wearing doesn't slip down around your neck. You might get your leg through it and choke yourself to death." He reached into his pocket and took out a quarter and tossed it on the table. "You've got yourself a herd of cows," he said. "If you want to be noble, take 'em and get to hell out of the country. From here on out I'll stay out of your affairs and you stay out of mine." He pushed the quarter across the table with his finger. "You bought me a drink the first day you came back," he said. "I'm paying for it. I wouldn't want you reminding me I'm obligated to you." He picked up a half-filled gunny sack of his belongings, turned abruptly and walked out of the door, leaving it open behind him. Watching him, Wayne saw Clyde swing angrily into the saddle and jerk at the pack horse's lead rope.

Wayne got up and stood in the doorway and watched his brother out of sight. He walked wearily back then and sat down at the table. He sat there a long time, staring at the quarter Clyde had left, trying to remember where it was that the relationship between himself and Clyde, never the best, had gone so completely off the rails. *It's a funny thing,* Wayne thought. *It's the man you try to help most that turns against you hardest.*

He remembered Brod Manwaring saying those very words to him a long time back. He hadn't known what Brod meant at the time; he did now. Brod had said those words the day he foreclosed on Beaver Creek.

The sound of a horse interrupted his

thoughts, and he was unsure of how much time had passed. He stood up, a puzzled frown pulling momentarily at his face muscles, then he stepped quickly across the room and picked up a rifle that was standing there in the corner. Peering through the window, he saw with a mixture of pleased surprise and irritation that it was Ruth Manwaring. He set the rifle back in the corner, only then realising that he had picked it up without even thinking about it. Opening the door, he stood there until she had ridden up, then said, "You after that cup of coffee I owe you already?"

"If I wanted a decent cup of coffee I wouldn't come here," she said. She was wearing a divided skirt and she dismounted gracefully. "Is Clyde here?"

"Just left," he said. "Which way did you come in?"

"I took the short cut past Newton's."

"That accounts for your missing him," Wayne said. "Clyde's moving down to the home place." He saw no reason to be elusive about it. It was done and Ruth would be the first to know, if not from him, then from Clyde.

"Did you do anything to talk him out of it?" she asked.

"I don't know," he said honestly. "Maybe I did, maybe I didn't. What's eating on him, Ruth?"

She seemed to avoid his question. "I had hoped I'd get here before Clyde left," she said. "I wanted the three of us to sit down and talk things out."

"No need for you to get mixed up in it, Ruth."

"How blind can you be, Wayne?" she said quietly.

There was an immediate unaccustomed awkwardness between them, and Wayne thought of Pete, the stableman, and his remark that he hated to see two brothers fighting over a woman. It hadn't been that, Wayne thought, and yet Ruth herself was saying it was. He said, "What's that kid been saying, Ruth?"

She looked at him with what he read as a trace of exasperation. "That he's tired of you calling him a kid, for one thing," Ruth said. She reached out and put a hand on Wayne's arm. "Let him live his own life. A man has to kill his own snakes, you know that."

"I didn't put Effinger and Calvin in jail," Wayne said. "Clyde did.

"No," Ruth said. "You did. You made an issue of it. What were you trying to prove?"

He found himself on the defensive and he didn't like it. "It wasn't a case of proving anything," he said. "If it had been an honest game—"

"Quit talking around it, Wayne," she said. "I'm talking about a man's dignity, not the right or wrong of a poker game or the price of a few steers. I'm talking about a man walking around with a big sign on his back that says, 'Don't touch me or my big brother will bite you.' That's what you've put on his back, Wayne, and he's been wearing it all his life. Except for the five years you were away, he's never had one thing that wasn't handed down by you, after you were through with it." He saw the tiredness and resignation in her eyes. "That's right," she said. "We're thinking it, so why not say it? Even I was handed down to him after you were through."

"That's a hell of a thing to say, Ruth."

"The truth often is."

He looked at her and felt the old pain that he had thought was gone and forgotten, and for a moment it was as freshly alive as it had ever been. There was something that had never been said and it needed saying. "I wanted something to offer you, Ruth," he said. "I figured maybe over the hill, some place, I'd make it." He felt the old tiredness. "I didn't want you to ever wonder whether it was you or Anvil I wanted to marry, Ruth," he said quietly.

She looked at him a long time and although there was anger in her eyes there was something else and he knew it was pity, and he knew too that he had never had anyone feel pity for him before. It was a weakening feeling. She said, "I won't slap your face, Wayne. But I doubt if I'll ever hear a worse insult."

He reached out suddenly and gripped both her arms. "I didn't mean it to be and you know it," he said roughly.

"So that's what it is you have against Mike Conaway, is it?" she said.

His hands relaxed and she moved away from him and turned to look off toward the hills, her arms folded across her breasts. "I'm glad we talked, Wayne," she said quietly. "I'm free now. Free to be honest with Clyde."

There was no thought of his brother in him now nor of Mike Conaway nor of any other tangible thing. There was only Ruth and himself and the memory of dreams and the false pride that had kept those dreams from fulfilment. He went to her and turned her roughly toward him, drawing her close, feeling her in his arms as he had before, and only then did he force himself to realize he had no right. . . . He let her go, but not until he had bent swiftly and touched his lips to her forehead. "It was wrong, Ruth. All wrong. If I had it all to do over—"

"But you can't have, can you, Wayne?" she said. "What's done is done." She turned from him then and he offered her no help as she mounted her horse. She rode away immediately, down the trail toward the home place, the trail toward Clyde.

The little calf Wayne had brought in that morning came wobbling out of the shed, bawled demandingly, and the mother cow answered. The calf bleated out his accusation of parental neglect, then went to the cow and, standing on wide-spread legs, started butting out its supper. The warm milk frothed from the corners of its mouth.

CHAPTER
8

CLYDE HARDESTY MET Mike Conaway by accident in town that evening and the two of them rode out to Anvil together.

In some ways, Clyde and Mike were alike. They were both exceptionally handsome men, openly friendly with others, but still quietly reserved. As well as they knew each other, they had actually talked little of their own personal affairs, and now, pressed by their own worries, they were even more silent as they rode through the darkness toward the lights of Anvil.

Arriving at the ranch, they passed a few comments about the weather with Tex Blanchard, and Mike spoke briefly about the business of Anvil.

"Charley was in today to pick up supplies," Tex said. "Half the crew's camped over around Wild Horse and the rest of 'em are in the Burnt Country. Says as far as they can tell now, the stock wintered fine. Not much drifting. Looks like about two weeks to branding time."

"Good," Mike said. "What did you find out about that sorrel mare?"

"Picked up a rock is all," Tex said. "She'll be all right."

Mike didn't answer. He went on toward the house and came alongside Clyde near the porch. "You going to see Brod?" Mike asked.

"Just stop in and say hello," Clyde said.

"I'll go on up to the house and tell Mercy I'm back, then," Mike said.

Clyde stood there a moment, watching Mike walk toward the white house, then he went on up to the house and tried the front door. It was locked. He knocked and waited, then seeing no light in the main section of the house, decided Ruth was probably in visiting with Brod. He went on down the porch and knocked on Brod's door, entering when Brod answered.

He always felt uneasy, trying to visit with Brod, in spite of the fact that Brod had never shown him anything but the utmost friendliness. He mildly resented Brod's gruff manner, but more than that, Clyde resented the fact that he always completely failed to talk Brod's language. He had never left Brod without thinking back on something that had been said, wondering why it hadn't been said differently. Whatever he said to Brod, Clyde habitually rephrased it the moment he was away from Brod.

Clyde stood there now, the greetings between himself and the old man finished, the awkward lag already apparent in their conversation. Clyde said, "I thought maybe Ruth was in here."

"Didn't you see her?" Brod said. "She

went into town about noon. Aims to spend the night with Gwen Perkins."

"Wish I had known it," Clyde said. "I was up at the cabin. Didn't get to town until late."

"That's part of being a cattle man," Brod said. "Cows first, pleasure second."

Immediately Clyde read something into the remark that wasn't there. "Ruth's the type that would see to it her husband took care of business," Clyde said. Immediately he wondered why he had made his answer that way. He would rephrase it a dozen ways later.

He saw Brod's old eyes searching his face. Brod said, "Clyde, I don't make it a practice to pry into a man's affairs. I wouldn't now, if I didn't consider you a part of my family."

"You mean the trouble between me and Wayne," Clyde said.

"A thing like that starts a lot of loose talk," Brod said. "I'd rather hear it from you than second-hand."

How can I explain it to you when I can't explain it to myself? Clyde thought. He shrugged and said, "I guess we both got a bull-headed streak in us. I had a couple of drinks too many, got in a poker game and got skinned. Wayne said what he thought about it and I told him I didn't figure it was any of his business. One thing led to another."

There was mild amusement in Brod's eyes. "Did he whip yuh?" he said.

"Damned if I don't think he did," Clyde said, and he somehow felt he was closer to Brod Manwaring right that moment than he had ever been before in his life. He said, "Glad you're feeling better, Brod. If Ruth's in town, I'll go on back in."

"Do it," Brod said. "What's a ride like that when a man's courtin'?"

"See you later then," Clyde said.

He went back out into the darkness and on an impulse turned and walked up toward the white house. Mercy opened the door to his knock, and for a moment she stood there in the door, letting her eyes adjust to the darkness. Clyde looked past her and said, "Mike here?"

"Oh, Clyde!" she said, pleased. "He went over to tell Tex something he had forgotten. After that he said he wanted to visit with Dad a while. Won't you come in? Coffee's hot."

He went inside, removing his hat immediately. She came and took the hat from his hand and hung it on the hall tree. "We might as well sit in the kitchen," she said.

116

"Might as well."

She fixed him coffee and they sat there, the self-consciousness growing between them. "I'm very happy, Clyde," she said softly.

If you were, you wouldn't have to say so, he thought immediately. He looked at her thinking, *I know you a lot better than I know Ruth,* wondering what had made him think that. "Your husband's a sharp businessman," he said finally. "He signed Wayne and the others up to a lease on Beaver Creek today."

"I don't know as I like to see him taking advantage of you and Wayne," she said.

"Not me," Clyde said. "I've pulled out of it." He saw her quick surprise and said immediately, "I was never cut out for the cow business, Mercy. You know that."

"I don't know any such thing," Mercy said. "You're just upset, Clyde. Everything will look better in the morning."

Sure, he thought *Every day in every way I'm getting better and better.* "Forget it, Mercy," he said. "I was just feeling sorry for myself." He stood up. "Thanks for the coffee."

"Clyde," she said, putting her hand on his arm, "I'm sorry you and Wayne had trouble."

"Don't be," he said. "Maybe it was good for both of us." He went to the door and opened it and looked out into the night. Half turning he said, "I guess I missed Ruth. Brod said she went in to spend the night with Gwen Perkins."

"That's a shame, Clyde," Mercy said. "She left quite early. She took the west trail. She thought she'd find you and Wayne at the cabin."

"It's all right," he said.

He went out, closing the door behind him, and as he walked toward his horse Mercy watched him and thought. *He doesn't act like a man who's about to be married.* She closed the door and went back inside, momentarily depressed, and then she remembered Wayne's advice that a woman could grow old worrying about nothing.

She took the two cups to the sink and washed them, humming a little tune, but the worry persisted. Was Clyde really in love with Ruth? Or did he know now that he would never own her completely—that part of Ruth would always belong to Wayne? Mercy was suddenly lonely. She wished Mike would come back. She wanted to talk. And yet it was so difficult to talk to Mike about Ruth and Wayne. . . . It was difficult, she realized, to talk to Mike about anything. Immediately she thought, *Where have I failed you, Mike?*

Coming across from the bunkhouse, Mike Conaway saw Clyde saying good night to Mercy. He waited a moment there in the darkness until Clyde had mounted and ridden down toward the gate, then he crossed on over to the porch of the main house and went directly to Brod's room.

"Ah, Mike," Brod said in greeting. "Sit down, son. Sit down."

"Glad you're still awake, Brod," Mike said. He reached into his inside coat pocket and took out the lease form and handed it across to Brod without comment.

Brod opened the paper, held it out at arm's length and moved it back and forth to adjust it to his vision. After a moment he folded the lease into its original creases and handed it back. "Pretty steep terms, ain't it?" Brod said.

"When I first went to work for you," Mike said, "you told me the price of anything depended on how bad somebody wanted it. Those boys wanted Beaver Creek pretty bad."

"I guess they did," Brod chuckled.

"The way I see it," Mike said, "We're actually loaning them money. We're gambling on their having a sure sale for their herd. We get paid when they sell." Mike watched the old man's expression. Mike had figured this out carefully. He had hoped to freeze Wayne out by driving a hard bargain, but in addition, he had been careful to remind Brod often that he, Mike, was only doing exactly what Brod himself would have done under similar circumstances. He knew Brod had no respect whatsoever for Leatherman, Faull and Newton; he could always hide behind that. At the same time he was showing Brod that he was man enough to put even Wayne Hardisty in a corner.

"Well, maybe you're right," Brod said. "You can't let 'em walk on you, that's sure. The more you give that kind, the more they expect you to give them." He excluded Wayne immediately by adding, "As for Wayne, he'd drive as hard a bargain if the tables were turned."

Mike relaxed. Brod's remark about Wayne was meant as a compliment to Wayne's business acumen, Mike knew. It was also a left-handed compliment to Mike, for Mike had backed Wayne down.

Brod was silent a moment. "Had a good

talk with Wayne yesterday morning," he said finally.

Mike felt that quick grab of fear he had felt so constantly since Wayne's return. He had awakened with it in the middle of the night, sitting bolt upright in bed. It was a fear that was twice as great because it was a fear of the unknown. There wasn't one tangible thing Wayne Hardisty could say against Mike. And yet there was such an accumulation of things that, properly presented, could almost certainly convince Brod that Mike Conaway had no intentions of spending the rest of his life running Anvil. . . . The fact that Mike had run out on a woman before. The dirty business of the Indian girl— even though Mercy knew about it—even though the authorities had cleared Mike completely. The truth was, Wayne Hardisty had cleared Mike of nothing, and Wayne Hardisty and Brod Manwaring thought a lot alike. . . . There was a dryness in Mike's mouth, but he controlled his expression and grinned lazily. He said, "Wayne try to put the pressure on you, did he?"

"He tried," Brod said.

"He's a stubborn son of a gun," Mike said, using Brod's own method of compliment. Mike was always careful not to run Wayne down in front of Brod, for he had immediately sensed the strong tie that existed between these two men. He had known of it long before he came to Oregon; he had seen it in the bluff, derogatory manner Wayne always used when speaking of Brod, this same left-handed damning that was as strong a compliment as one man could give another. Mike had seen it again when he had drifted into this country as if by accident and landed a job with Anvil. He had counted on it, and it was here, for his news of Wayne and his avowed friendship for Wayne had been the open sesame to this job, just as he had been sure it would be.

"It won't hurt Wayne to crawl a few times," Brod said, almost as if to himself. "It'll rub off the rough corners of that damn bull-neck pride of his." Brod sighed. "You know, Mike," he said, "it's a wearisome state of affairs when a man has to lose a lot of the starch that made him a man before he can call himself grown up."

Mike agreed, and the conversation shifted to talk of the roundup and the condition of the cattle. Mike was careful to mention small details, such as the sorrel mare that had gone lame and some lumber he had ordered for some new chutes. "Figgered I'd go over to the Burnt Country in the morning," Mike said. "Spend a couple of days with the boys there and then maybe cut back along Timber Creek and join up with the other crew."

"You learn a country fast, Mike," Brod said.

"I'm not afraid to ask questions," Mike said.

Brod was thoughtful. "It hasn't been easy, has it, boy?" he said.

"I knew it wouldn't be," Mike said. "Mercy and I both knew it. We knew what folks around here would say. We decided if we loved each other enough it wouldn't make any difference."

"You're doing a good job, boy," Brod said. That old roughness came into his voice. "Clyde and Ruth set a date yet?"

"If they have, they haven't said so," Mike said, mildly surprised at this sudden turn. "Why?"

"Like to see things settled, that's all," Brod said. "I spent my life building up Anvil. It's like a part of me. I want to know the girls will be taken care of after I'm gone."

Again Mike felt that dryness of mouth, the pounding of his pulse in his temples. He had to be easy now, but this was the time. He said, "I'm counting strong on getting a good price for those stockers, once I get 'em to Montana."

"Yeah," Brod said. "I've been giving that a lot of thought."

"You're in favour of it, aren't you?" Mike said, and was immediately worried that he had said that too fast.

"Sure," Brod said. "I think it's a smart idea. I was telling Ruth and Mercy this morning I thought it was our only out. We can't depend on the local market, the way things are, and it sure won't hurt us to get rid of some of our breeding stock. The way the market's been the last two years we're running way heavy to cows." He looked up suddenly. "How many you think we ought to go?"

Every damn head I can get away with, Mike thought, and said, "They'll take all the yearling steers we want to give 'em, I figure. Maybe a thousand head of heifers for their breeding stock. . . ."

"It's a hell of a drive," Brod said. "Wayne was telling me there's a stretch across Idaho after you leave the Snake where you're up to three days without water."

"That's so," Mike said, "but once you pass that you got grass and water all the way. They'll fatten on the trail." He gave Brod a quick glance. "It's all right if a man knows the country."

"Yeah," Brod said. "That's the thing." He steepled his hands and started tapping his fingers together. He looked up suddenly. "Given any thought to a trail boss, Mike?"

"Sure," Mike said, surprised at the question. "I've been over that country. I naturally figured I'd go along."

Brod nodded. "That's what's worrying me, Mike."

Fear built a vacancy in Mike's stomach. He laughed. "I can handle it, Brod."

"I know you can, Mike," Brod said. "Trouble is, I don't see how we can spare you here, do you? You got things pretty well under control."

"I figured Tex and Smiley and maybe Clayton and Brock best stay on here," Mike said carefully. Those four were permanent Anvil hands and Mike didn't want them along when he sold the herd in Montana. He could pay off the rest of the crew and they would mind their own business, but these old-timers, especially Tex, would be apt to get snoopy. . . .

"I'd rather you'd be here, Mike," Brod said. "I ain't foolin' myself. I might be gone in a month." He avoided Mike's eyes. "That's the reason I asked you about Ruth and Clyde. I was wonderin' if I could count on Clyde bein' here. I don't reckon I can. I'd feel a lot better knowin' you were here if I forgot to wake up some morning." He rubbed a bony hand across his mouth. "Ruth's as reliable as a man, but she ain't a man." He gave Mike a knowing grin. "Mercy would go to pieces."

"You'd be here, Brod," Mike said. "You're gonna be around a long time. I wouldn't trust anybody but myself to trail an Anvil herd that far."

"I was thinking of Wayne," Brod said. "He knows that country same as you."

Mike lowered his head and worked thoughtfully at squeezing a splinter in the ball of his thumb. He had trouble holding his hands steady. Here was a development he hadn't foreseen, a development he couldn't let happen. If Wayne Hardisty bossed that herd, Mike Conaway's plans were finished. He would be stuck here on Anvil with Mercy for another year at least before he could make up another herd. He thought, *What's the matter, you old devil? Don't you trust me? Has Wayne said something?* He said finally, "I doubt if Wayne

126

would be interested. He's got his own herd to think about."

"He'd do it if I asked him," Brod said.

He'd not only do it, he'd jump at the chance, Mike thought. Those few cows Wayne had of his own would take care of themselves on Beaver Creek. *Careful,* he thought. *Careful what you say. Give yourself time to think it out.* . . . He said, "I hadn't thought of it, Brod. It's an idea, anyway." He had to know how far this had gone. "You mention it to Wayne, did you?"

"Not yet," Brod said. "I wanted to see what you thought first. I'll talk to him about it."

Damned if you will, Mike thought, and immediately there was perspiration on his upper lip, for the thought that he would have to kill Wayne Hardisty had crossed his mind and lay there for a moment so vividly strong that he had been almost afraid Brod could see it. He stood up, feeling a shakiness in his knees that he couldn't control. He said, "I guess I better let you get some sleep, Brod." He turned and started toward the door and Brod's thin voice stopped him.

"One thing more, Mike," Brod said.

"Yeah, Brod?"

"I'm leaving Anvil half and half to Ruth

and Mercy," Brod said. "That means you and Clyde, even if it don't say so in black and white." His voice was gruff. "I'm willing Beaver Creek to Wayne Hardisty."

Mike reached out and gripped the door jamb. "The whole of it?"

"The whole of it," Brod said. "If Wayne's dad had had anything but calf slobbers for a backbone it would have belonged to Wayne anyway. It never was part of Anvil. It's range we don't need. If cows' legs keep gettin' shorter the day will come when all a man needs for a ranch is a horse pasture. Wayne's wanted that range for his own from the time he was big enough to ride. I always planned on giving it to Wayne and Ruth for a wedding present. That didn't work out, but I still want Wayne to have it."

For one of the first times in his life Mike Conaway had a bad time controlling his expression. He half stepped through the door, thankful for the outside darkness. "It's a damn fine present, Brod," Mike said. "Only thing is, I'm not sure Wayne wants to settle down. If he had of, him and Ruth would have been married, the way you planned."

"That wasn't a case of settlin' down," Brod said. "That was a case of that damn bull-neck pride. He didn't have sense enough to see it would have been worth all of Anvil to me to have him for a son-in-law." Brod was seized by a fit of coughing and Mike stood there, wanting to run, wanting to get the devil away from here. Brod got his breath and said, "He'll make you a good neighbour, Mike. You said a while ago you wasn't afraid to ask questions. If you get in trouble, don't be afraid to ask Wayne. The run-in you two had will blow over. It has with you. It will with Wayne." He coughed again. "Good night, Mike."

"Good night, Brod," Mike Conaway said.

He stepped into the darkness and for a moment he stood there, staring at the lights in the white house. The stars were whirling at him, bombarding him. He thought of Wayne, delivering that herd to Montana, collecting all that money and riding straight back here to turn it over to Ruth and Mercy. And he thought of Wayne living here beside him, for ever, constantly looking at him with that knowing half smile. *He's got me trapped, damn it,* he thought savagely. *As long as Wayne Hardisty is alive, I'm trapped.*

He thought of Lorry Calvin and Rudy Effinger, and the worry about what Brod and Wayne would say when they found out Mike had bailed these two out was again pressing. He started walking toward the white house, the conviction that he had to get rid of Wayne Hardisty dinning in his brain. He fought against saying it or admitting it to himself, but it was always there. There was no other way.

You've got to kill him, Mike Conaway, the inner voice said, *because there's no other way to get rid of him now. You've got to kill him and you haven't got the guts to do it.*

CHAPTER
9

FOUR DAYS IN jail did quite a bit for Rudy Effinger's battered face but it did nothing at all for his temper. He stalked out of Don Lien's office and glared at the town of Three Rivers, defying anyone to make a remark. In contrast, Lorry Calvin lazed along and took time to enjoy the spring sun. He tipped his hat to a woman he passed and stopped in at the cigar store to thank the proprietor for having sent tobacco over to the jail. He acted as if he had had no more than a pleasant vacation for himself, and in fact, he felt exactly that way.

Because he was a businessman, Lorry

went directly to the slaughterhouse with Effinger. He had a pretty good thing shaping up, Lorry Calvin figured, but then, the contract he and Rudy had to supply beef to the Big Pine Lumber camps was a good thing, too. There was no sense burning an old bridge until the new bridge was built and tested, Lorry always figured.

Lorry watched, amused, while Rudy went into the storage room and sniffed and poked at the carcasses, hanging there. "At least they ain't spoiled," Rudy said. "No thanks to the Hardistys."

"I figured the meat would keep all right," Lorry said. They also supplied meat to the local butcher shop, and they had given the butcher a key and trusted him to cut his own meat during their sojourn in jail.

"Damn you, Calvin," Rudy exploded suddenly, "you act like you've got all the time in the world. Two more days of this sunshine the woods will be dried out and the camps will be running full blast. You realize we've got a contract to take care of?"

The wrinkles deepened at the corners of Lorry Calvin's eyes, the only indication of amusement in his mask-like smile. "You've got six beeves coming from Hardisty," he said.

"To hell with that," Effinger said gruffly. "I'll take care of Wayne Hardisty later."

Calvin gave his soundless laugh. "I'll bet you four bits you don't," he said.

Effinger's dark face was purple with anger. "I'm sick of the whole thing," he said. "We need some beef, and we need it now."

Calvin took a match from his pocket and worked it between his wide-spaced front teeth. He was leaning casually against the wall. "We'll get it from Mike Conaway," he said.

"At his price?" Effinger said.

Calvin shook his head. "At our price."

"What the hell makes you think you got Conaway buffaloed?"

"We're out, ain't we?"

"Listen, Lorry," Rudy Effinger said. "You're playing that game on your own, see? If you think you can bluff Mike Conaway, hop to it. I don't want no part of it."

"You want some beef, don't you?"

"Hell, yes, I want some beef."

"We'll get some," Lorry Calvin said. "Quit worrying about it." He turned and started to leave.

"Where you think you're going?" Effinger said.

"To get my gun from Don Lien," Calvin

said. "He had to go get it from wherever it is he keeps things like that."

"You better leave that thing alone," Effinger said. "It's got us into enough trouble."

Calvin turned slowly, his eyes expressionless, heavy-lidded, sleepy. "You give and you take, Rudy," he said mildly. "A gun's got me out of trouble a lot more times than it ever got me in." He strolled through the office, pausing to glance idly at some mail on the desk, then he went outside and sauntered down the street, whistling softly. He thought of the beating Wayne Hardisty had given Rudy Effinger and he was genuinely amused. *That's really trying to make it the hard way,* he thought, *playing with the Hardistys. If you had everything they owned and them to boot you wouldn't have anything. But Mike Conaway and Anvil. . . .* There was something worth going for.

He went down to the marshal's office and had to wait a full half-hour. He was pleasantly humble and apologetic when he asked Don Lien for his gun.

The little valley around Wayne Hardisty's cabin had taken on the appearance of a full-scale cattle ranch. For four days now, Wayne, Leatherman, Faull and Newton had been bringing Wayne's stock out of the canyons, moving them down to the feed lot proper, and now they were bunched there, a bawling, discontented mass composed of everything from week-old calves to a couple of range-wise bulls long past their usefulness.

Sitting on the corral fence, a battered tally book in his hand, Wayne scratched his head, wet a stubby pencil on his tongue and figured up the total for the second time. "Looks like about two hundred head of Cleggs," he said. Clegg was the name of the Montana buyer and they had started designating stock they knew Clegg would accept as "Cleggs". "Runs a little short, don't it?"

"Trouble with you, Hardisty," Leatherman said, "you're so used to workin' on book count you double-crossed your own self."

"I jumped a couple of deer this morning," Faull said. "Sure you didn't count them in, Wayne?"

"Wonder if I could get away with it?" Wayne said. "I could tell Clegg it's a new breed of Oregon cow."

"I wouldn't doubt you'd try it," Faull said.

"You catch up a couple of bucks and brand 'em and I will," Wayne said. He shrugged. "Might as well cut the Cleggs out right now." Clegg wanted breeding stock, his preference being yearling heifers, and he had been willing to pay top price for them, but he had known and expected that he would get some younger, some older. Wayne glanced over the bunched herd and again had that dragging down feeling of just getting by. His end of the bargain with his partners had been two hundred and fifty head. He was going to have to cut deeply into his own breeding stock to meet the commitment. *Another deal like this and I'll be out of business,* he mused, and immediately thought of Mike Conaway. *And wouldn't you like that?* he thought.

It wasn't a case of miscalculation or of going into this deal blind. When Wayne and Leatherman, Faull and Newton had first decided on it, they had had an option on plenty of grass at a price that would have let them come out with a good profit. Wayne had known he would have to strip his own herd, but he hadn't cared. Since the closing of the mines, eastern Oregon ranges were heavily overstocked. Wayne had figured that with the profits from this deal he could move quietly before the news of the new Montana and Wyoming markets spread and buy up stockers of his own from any one of a dozen small outfits whose owners were anxious to get out of the failing cattle business. But the owner of the graze they had intended to lease had made a sudden decision to go into the sheep business. It wasn't a case of offering more for the grass; it was a case of not being able to get it at any price. It was then Mike Conaway offered them Beaver Creek, and knowing Wayne and the others had no choice, it was then Mike had tried to force Wayne out. The trouble was, Wayne had recognized the move for what it was, and knowing Mike, he had stubbornly refused to budge.

Wayne resented the worrying thought, for the past four days had been completely pleasant. Riding with Leatherman and Faull and Newton, he had discovered depths to them and a sense of humour in them that he had never suspected. There was something about working cattle that brought out the best in a man, Wayne always thought, and he had found it so here. They were small men and they thought small, but there was a solidness about them, and their concern for the welfare of their families and what little they owned was stronger because of its smallness.

They had worked early and late, not going home at night but bunking here with Wayne at the cabin. With the smell of brewing coffee and the blue haze of cigarette smoke in the little room, Wayne had found himself becoming one with these three men and he had liked the feeling. A man didn't need to be alone. Not if he stood still and went after what he wanted. A drifter was always alone.

He had come to place a lot of importance on that sense of aloneness, Wayne saw, and he knew it had been with him since the day he had left Three Rivers, five years back. He hadn't gone out to find something better, regardless of how often he told himself he had. He had run away from his responsibilities. Mostly he had run away from Ruth, not man enough to offer himself for what he was, letting her make the decision. It wasn't a flattering thing to admit, but it was the truth, and once a man faced it he could make his decision. Wayne had made his. He was here to stay.

He had returned here because of his father's death, and now he remembered back to the savage anger that had struck him when he had first learned of Mike

Conaway's marriage to Mercy Manwaring. It was so obviously a marriage of convenience for Mike. Wayne had always felt like a big brother toward Mercy. And so, his immediate decision had been to expose Mike for what he was, a completely unscrupulous fortune-hunter. It would only be Wayne's word against Mike's, but Wayne intended to try it. But the very first time he had seen Mercy and Mike Conaway together he had known he wouldn't go through with it.

They made a handsome pair, Mercy and Mike. Mercy radiantly happy, Mike already solidly established in the community, Brod, a dying man, contented with the knowledge that he had a son-in-law to carry on with Anvil. And there was Ruth and Clyde. . . . He knew then for certain that destroying Mike would be more permanently humiliating to Mercy and Brod and Ruth than it would be to Mike himself. These people were a permanent part of this place. They would have to live here and live with the gossip that he, Wayne, could start. Mike could run away from it. The others couldn't.

But his lack of respect and his deep, though unprovable conviction that Mike Conaway had actually been responsible for the death of that Indian girl had been like an obligation on his mind, refusing to let him leave. *I'm staying, Mike,* he had decided. *Maybe you've changed. I hope you have. Play it straight and I'll leave you alone. Step over the line once and you'll know I'm here.* He hadn't told Mike that. Mike had known.

Wayne climbed down from the fence now and glanced at the sun, saying to Leatherman, "We might as well eat before we start moving the first bunch down to Beaver Creek, hadn't we?"

"If we don't you're gonna be short of a hand," Leatherman said. "My belly thought my throat was cut two hours ago."

"Somebody will have to stick here and see they don't start drifting back up the canyon," Wayne said. "Whose turn is it?

"Not mine," Leatherman said. "That's for damn sure."

"Hey, Faull," Wayne called. "You want to keep an eye on 'em while the rest of us eat?"

"Why me?" Faull said. "Newton ain't done nothin' but sleep to noon and knock off work at one since this started."

"Well, will you look who's talking?" Newton said. "I do believe it's Mister Faull. I didn't recognize him without a fork full of grub in front of his face."

"How about you, Hardisty?" Faull said.

"You think ownin' these cows is all you got to do?"

"I'm dyin' of hunger," Lee Leatherman said. "Right here in the saddle I'm dyin'."

"We'll draw straws for it," Wayne said. "Long straw eats last." He rode close, reached out and took four matches from Leatherman's hat-band. He bit off the ends of two, then concealing the four in his hand so only the heads were showing, he held them out to Leatherman.

Lee drew, looked at the match and said, "I got a short one. The end's busted off."

Wayne turned in the saddle, grinning now, and offered the matches to Newton, who took one. "Me too," Newton said, "Mine's short."

"Guess you're stuck, Bob," Wayne drawled, showing two full-length matches to Faull.

"Hey, wait a minute," Faull said. "There's two long ones. How about you, Hardisty?"

"Why, I'm the boss, Bob," Wayne said. He reined his horse and heard Leatherman's and Newton's shouted laughter rising above Faull's howled complaints.

They were halfway through their meal of canned pork and beans and steaks from a buck Wayne had killed the first day of the roundup, when they heard a rider approaching. "Now who in the devil would that be?" Wayne said. He got up and went to the window, then spoke across his shoulder. "It's Tex Blanchard. What do you suppose that old he-goat wants?"

"I guess Brod fired him again," Lee said through a mouthful of food. "Probably wants a job."

"He never gets further than the bunkhouse door when Brod fires him," Wayne said. He went to the door and called, "Put a sack over your head, Tex. That ugly face of yours will dry up every cow in my herd."

"Just watch your sass, youngster," Tex said. "You push your luck with me and I'll cut your herd and dwindle it down to size. It's probably half Anvil anyway."

"Go ahead and cut 'em," Wayne said "You couldn't see a brand anyway. I'm surprised you can see the cows."

"There's four I can't see," Tex said, swinging out of his saddle. There was a note of seriousness in his voice. He stood there a moment, a bandy-legged little man, as wiry as a crow. "Serious now," he said. "Did you run into any Anvil drift?"

"Not a one," Wayne said. "Why? You missing some?"

"I had four spotted in a draw back of Leatherman's," Tex said. "Don't know how the devil they got separated off up that way. Went over to pick 'em up just now and they weren't there."

"Probably over in that meadow back of Faull's place," Wayne said.

Tex shook his head. "I looked. If you ain't seen 'em, they must of took off in the other direction."

"North?" Wayne said. "There's nothing up that way to attract a cow."

"Nothing but that old horse camp Lorry Calvin and Rudy Effinger used to keep up," Tex said.

"If Lorry and Rudy weren't in jail I'd tell you where your cows were," Wayne said.

"They're not in jail, Wayne," Tex Blanchard said. "They got out this morning."

All humour left Wayne Hardisty's eyes. "Did Clyde bail 'em out?"

"I don't know who bailed 'em out," Tex said. "I ain't been in town. But they're out. I saw 'em this morning." Tex's eyes were worried. "What do you think, Wayne?"

"I think maybe we better ride up and take a look," Wayne said.

CHAPTER
10

WAYNE SADDLED A fresh horse while Tex went in and helped himself to a plate of beans and a venison steak and talked briefly with Leatherman and Newton. When Leatherman came out to relieve Faull, Wayne glanced at him and saw the worry on Lee's face. "You have to get mixed up in it, Wayne?" Lee asked.

"Just giving a neighbour a hand," Wayne said.

"Let Anvil take care of their own chores," Lee advised. "They've got a dozen hands."

"They're on a roundup," Wayne said.

Lee said bleakly, "What is it you want to find, Wayne? Four Anvil steers, or Lorry Calvin?"

"I guess that'll depend on Lorry Calvin," Wayne said. He mounted and rode the short distance to the cabin and called Tex. Then, glancing at Tex's horse, he saw the butt of a carbine protruding from a saddle scabbard. *I don't want it to happen,* he thought, *but I'd be a fool to think it couldn't.* He swung down and went into the cabin and got the six-shooter he had bought at the Emporium.

Mildly self-conscious, he turned his back to Tex and Newton. He loaded five chambers and thrust the gun into the waistband of his trousers. He was wearing a short denim jacket and he buttoned it so that it concealed the butt of the gun, but the bulge of the weapon was obvious. "If we want to get up there before dark we better get at it," he said to Tex. He went back and mounted and rode on, not waiting for Tex.

He hadn't thought it the least bit strange that Tex had come to him to ask for help. They were old friends and Tex had sense enough to know that if his hunch was right it wouldn't do to go riding in on Lorry Calvin and Rudy Effinger by himself.

Tex overtook Wayne shortly and reined in alongside him. Without turning his head Wayne said, "How's Brod?"

"Not good, Wayne," Tex said.

Wayne felt a sadness, knowing that something passed out of a country when men like Brod died. He said idly, "Who in hell would want to see Lorry and Rudy out of jail?"

"I wondered the same," Tex said "I can't figure it."

They cut close to Newton's place and

Wayne said, "I'll swing by and tell Newton's wife Newt will be home tonight." He reined left and came to the house, and Mrs. Newton, a pan of dish water in her hands, stood there and talked to him a moment. She threw the dish water into the yard and a half-dozen chickens came over and picked idly at the mud.

"I'll send one of my boys to tell Edith and Wilma," she said, naming Faull's and Leatherman's wives.

"We'll gather your stock next," Wayne said. "That'll keep your old man home a few days."

"That ain't no particular joy," Mrs. Newton said.

Wayne laughed dutifully, then went back and joined Tex. The two men put their horses into a fast trot and in time came to the canyon where Tex had first spotted the four Anvil strays. Tex leaned down and pointed to a trail in the new grass. The track of the four steers was plain, as was the sign of two horses.

"Maybe Mike and one of the boys picked them up," Wayne said.

"Mike's been on roundup," Tex said. "If any of the boys had picked them up, they would have brought 'em on in."

They rode on up the canyon, away from Leatherman's place and on to Anvil range and intersected the well-defined trail that led back into Anvil's foothill range. Pausing here a moment to check tracks, Wayne caught the sound of an approaching rider. He had dismounted and was squatted down, looking at the ground, and now he turned and saw Mike Conaway coming down the trail toward him. Mike hadn't shaved in four days and he sat his saddle like a man who had been working his share and more. *There's no law against a man changing,* Wayne thought. *Maybe you have. . . .* Mike reined up surprised at seeing Wayne and Tex there. He said, "What the devil did you lose?"

"Nothing," Wayne said. "You lost four steers."

"How you figure that?" Mike asked.

Tex gave him the story quickly and a frown settled between Mike's eyes. "A lot of guess work," he said. "Those steers are probably within a half a mile of here."

Again Mike felt that horrible pressing in feeling that had kept growing and growing. Mike knew where those four steers were. He himself had sold them to Lorry and Effinger. "Thanks for looking into it, anyway, Wayne," he said.

"I've got cows of my own," Wayne said. "If somebody will steal your cows, they'll steal mine."

"I don't believe they're stolen," Mike said.

"We can find out," Wayne said. "Want to come along?"

"No," Mike said. "Why should I?"

"You boss Anvil, don't you?" Wayne said.

Every place I turn you stick your nose in my affairs, Hardisty, Mike thought savagely. *And it will always be that way as long as you're around, and if you inherit Beaver Creek you'll be around for ever. . . .* "I got to get on home," he said. "Brod's expecting me."

"He'd expect you to look after his stock, too," Wayne said. Wayne mounted and he and Tex rode on.

Mike waited there a moment, watching them ride off, and he thought suddenly, *I'm playing this wrong. I'm not acting like a man who's going to own half of Anvil. I wouldn't want it to get back to Brod that I refused to go after my own beef. Besides, I can't let Wayne talk to Lorry.* He turned his horse then and called, "If you're so set on it, I'll go along. I still think you're crazy."

"We'll find out," Wayne said.

The trail of the missing steers became increasingly difficult to follow as they rode up the canyon that narrowed between multi-coloured sandstone cliffs, their varying colours sharp in the brilliant sunlight. A mile into the canyon a winter run-off had spread a delta of sand some eight or ten feet across, and here the tracks were plainly visible. Looking down at the imprint left by shod horses, Wayne said, "Satisfied, Mike?" Catching Mike's reluctant nod, he added, "They'd go on out the canyon and around the end of the butte there. We might as well climb out of here and cut across. We'll save ourselves an hour."

The climb out of the gorge and on to the plateau was a rugged one and not one that two men driving four steers would attempt. Tex and Mike and Wayne gave their full attention to the climb and when they reached the top all three horses were blowing heavily. They stopped there a moment and, watching Wayne, Mike thought, *You like trouble, don't you?*

Mike had held back and now Wayne and Tex were ahead of him, their backs to him. Mike's hand dropped down to the holstered gun he was wearing, a practice followed by most of the men when they were on roundup. *Why don't I kill you and get it over with?* he thought bleakly. *There's no other way. . . .*

Wayne turned in his saddle then and smiled. "Quite a climb," he said.

Mike felt as weak and shaken as if he had actually committed the act instead of just thinking about it, and he knew certainly that he wouldn't have had the strength to lift that gun from his holster. There was no way to explain his inability. He only knew it was so. He felt a complete desolation as they rode across the high plateau studded with wind-swept juniper and clusters of sage.

There was a gradual rise to the ground now, an increasing stand of long-needle bull pine, and beyond here the hills rose smoothly into timbered slopes of pine. This was still Anvil range, and although it was the section closest to the ranch headquarters, it was the section Mike knew least, for the winter range lay south and west of here, its border backing against the small layouts owned by Leatherman, Faull and Newton. The Hardisty place was at the far south end of the valley, running east and west; Beaver Creek adjoined it on the east, a long, narrow stem of land that ran from the Hardisty place up the Beaver Creek valley, mushrooming out to over a full section of splendid grass where Beaver Creek forked. At this place they were no more than six miles in a direct line from Anvil headquarters at the north end of Three Rivers valley, some twelve miles from the town itself. Lorry Calvin's abandoned horse-camp, Mike knew, was just over the next rise. Talk had it that the main reason the camp was abandoned was because of its proximity to Brod Manwaring's back yard.

Mike felt an increasing dread as they approached their destination. He had been a fool to bail Lorry and Rudy out, he knew now, but what other out was there? And yet, it had solved nothing, for here he was in deeper than ever. He looked again at Wayne's back and put the blame squarely where he felt it belonged.

He saw Wayne rein up at the top of the rise and he heard the confidence in Wayne's voice, and it was as irritating as the confidence Mike had heard in Lorry Calvin's voice there at the jail. "There's your steers, Mike," Wayne said.

They could look directly down on to the dilapidated shack and the half-collapsed juniper-pole corral. There was no sign of Calvin or Effinger, but two saddled horses cropped at the grass that was growing in the unused corral. Just beyond the corral the four steers grazed contentedly. An "A" frame scaffold, rigged with block and tackle, stood in front of the shack.

"Looks like they aimed to butcher 'em right here," Tex observed.

"There's an old road runs back in towards the Big Pines camps," Wayne said. "Fellow that had this place when I was a kid used to cut cordwood back there in the hills and haul it out that way."

Tex reached down and took his carbine from its saddle scabbard and levered in a shell. "I'd rather Effinger would do his slaughtering in town," Tex said. "Makes it easier to keep an eye on him."

"Why don't we tell him so?" Wayne said. He turned and there was a questioning challenge in his eyes. "You coming, Mike?"

"Why wouldn't I?" Mike said. "They're my steers."

"They're Anvil, anyway," Wayne said.

They were within fifty yards of the shack when both Rudy Effinger and Lorry Calvin stepped outside. Calvin surveyed the riders quickly and turned as if intending to go into the cabin. "Stay put, Lorry," Wayne said casually. "The last time I let you wander off you found yourself a gun."

Wayne dismounted and Tex swung the rifle, idly covering Lorry and Effinger.

"Now what, Hardisty?" Calvin asked.

"Just lookin' around," Wayne said. "Those four steers over there got Anvil's brand on 'em by any chance?"

The smile on Lorry's face seemed to widen. "Go look," he said.

"I will," Wayne said.

He left his horse ground tied and walked around the corral, over toward the grazing steers. The four animals looked up suddenly and one glance at their earmarks alone told Wayne he had made a mistake. The steers bore the brand of Art Keyes, a small rancher over near Kinzua. Wayne turned, momentarily puzzled, then he glanced at the "A" frame and block and tackle. A swarm of blowflies buzzed angrily around the scuffed-up ground beneath the frame and Wayne had the answer. He walked idly across to the frame and started digging at the dust with his boot toe. Beneath the thin covering of new dirt the ground was saturated with blood. "Been doing a little butchering, have you, Rudy?" Wayne asked.

"Why not?" Effinger said. "I own a slaughterhouse."

There was amusement in Calvin's voice.

"What brand did you find on those steers, Hardisty?" he asked.

They had Wayne where they wanted him, Lorry and Rudy figured. They had butchered four Anvil steers this morning but the meat was gone and Wayne would play the devil finding the hides and offal. Regardless of what Wayne knew, he had no proof. Rudy, enjoying this now, said, "Don't you remember, Lorry? That's the four I bought of Art Keyes." He reached into his pocket and took out a paper and handed it to Lorry. "There's the bill of sale on 'em."

"Maybe we ought to show it to Hardisty," Calvin said. "Hardisty thinks he's a policeman."

Wayne glanced at Tex and knew he could count on the old man, then he let his gaze drift to Mike Conaway. "Looks like they already butchered those four Anvil steers we trailed here, Mike," Wayne said. "You want cash for 'em or you want to just take those four by the corral?"

Mike, momentarily relieved by the turn this thing had taken, felt a surge of confidence. After all, they were his steers; he was rightly in charge here. He said, "I don't want either one, Hardisty. We haven't got anything against these men."

"Now you make sense, Conaway," Lorry Calvin said.

Mike saw the disgust in Wayne's eyes. "How you figure you'll explain it to Brod?" Wayne said.

"Listen, Hardisty," Mike Conaway said savagely. "I'll run Anvil."

"Into the ground, if you back down from these two," Wayne said. He half turned his head, still keeping an eye on Lorry Calvin. "What do you think, Tex?"

"I know what Brod would do if he was here," Tex Blanchard said.

"Tell Mike," Wayne said. "He's running Anvil."

"Brod would take those four steers," Tex said.

"So would I," Wayne said.

Lorry Calvin said, "Like you said to me, Hardisty. You'll whip me first."

"I figured on that," Wayne said. "You and me had some unfinished business anyway."

Lorry moved slightly, spreading his feet as if to brace himself. "Only this time it's you that's got the gun, is that it?"

Wayne had actually forgotten about the gun thrust in the waistband of his trousers. He gave Lorry a thorough glance, making sure the man was unarmed, then he unbuttoned his jacket, drew the gun and weighed it momentarily in his hand. He walked across then and handed the weapon to Tex. "You ever see a rib-kicker get kicked in the ribs, Tex?" Wayne asked.

"Not lately," Tex said.

"Keep Effinger out of it and you will," Wayne said. He turned then and met Mike's gaze directly. "Watch Mike too," he said to Tex. "Your boss seems to be a friend of these two."

From the tail of his eye, Wayne saw Lorry Calvin stoop and pick up something from the ground. Wayne turned and Lorry was rushing in at him. Too late, Wayne realized that Lorry had snatched up a three-foot length of wood from the clutter there in the yard.

CHAPTER

11

WAYNE THREW UP his arm and caught the impact of the club across the muscles of his left shoulder. It was a paralysing blow that sent him reeling backward and Calvin was after him again, the club raised. Wayne threw up both arms and caught the blow across the ribs and felt the breath spurt from his lungs. He retreated further, fighting to get his breath, and he collided solidly with the juniper-pole corral. Vaguely he heard Tex's reedy voice shouting, "Lay off, Calvin. Lay off or damn you I'll kill you!"

Calvin stopped flat-footed. His face was dead-white, his eyes brightly alive, his lips pulled away from his teeth. "Call off your dog, Hardisty," he said. "This was to be between you and me."

Wayne stood there a moment, panting heavily, pain stabbing through his chest with every breath. Slowly then he started moving along the corral fence, his eyes on a broken rail a few feet away. Lorry saw his objective and took two steps forward again Tex's voice stopped him.

Calvin stood his ground and watched Wayne stoop and pick up the length of juniper. It was bone-dry and as hard as iron, some four inches in diameter and approximately four feet long. One end had been neatly cut by an axe; the other end was sharp and jagged where it had been broken. Wayne hefted the club in his hand. "All right, Tex," he called. "Stay out of it like the man says." He moved in then, the club gripped solidly in his right hand.

He saw Calvin back away and thought, *You always play it with the odds in your favour, don't you? I'll remember that.* He rushed in, his club high, and saw Calvin throw up his own club to parry the blow. It was exactly what Wayne had wanted. Swinging his arm in a long, downward arc, he threw the entire weight of his body into it and smashed the club solidly against Lorry Calvin's legs. Lorry's legs went out from under him as if they had been cut off at the knees. He hit the ground face down and Wayne was on him. Shifting his grip on the club then, Wayne drove the jagged end of it savagely against the back of Lorry's right hand.

He heard Lorry's howl of pain, saw him lose his grip on his club, and Wayne tossed his own weapon aside. He got off Lorry's back, his hand gripping Calvin's shirt collar. For a moment they struggled, then Wayne was on his feet, dragging Lorry up with him. "Now," Wayne panted. "We'll play it my way." He shoved Lorry back with his left hand and hit him with his right.

Lorry's head jerked back but Wayne didn't release his left-hand grip on Calvin's shirt collar. He pulled Lorry close and hit him again and felt Calvin's knees sag. With a vicious, back-hand slap across the mouth,

Wayne let go of Calvin's shirt. Lorry slumped to the ground and lay there.

Wayne went to the corral fence and put his arms on the top rail. For a moment he stood there, his head down, getting control of his breathing. He turned then and faced Rudy Effinger. "I'm taking those four steers out there in place of the four you stole from Anvil," he said. "If you figure on stopping it, now's the time."

Rudy Effinger was strangely calm. "Go ahead and take 'em," he said. "That's plain, outright stealing. I got a bill of sale for those four. Go ahead and take 'em. I'll see you get six months to think it over, Hardisty. I'll have Sheriff Bud Stark on your tail so fast it will make your head spin."

"You do that, Rudy," Wayne said. He went over and retrieved his gun from Tex and thrust the weapon back in his waistband. He looked at Tex and said, "You afraid of Sheriff Bud Stark, Tex?"

"Six months in jail sounds good to me," Tex said. "I been meanin' to take some time off."

"Don't be a fool!" Mike Conaway said suddenly. "Effinger is right. If you take those four steers it's plain, outright stealing. I'll have no part of it."

Wayne looked at Mike and everything he knew and everything he suspected about the man was there in his eyes. "Don't, then," Wayne said. "Nobody asked you." He mounted his horse and heard Rudy Effinger cursing vilely and steadily while he and Tex rounded up the four steers and headed them up the slope toward Anvil range.

"You've cut your own throat this time, Hardisty!" Effinger shouted after them. He shook his first at their departing backs. "I'll see you rot in jail for this!"

Lorry Calvin was stirring there on the ground. Mike, visibly shaken, dismounted quickly and went over and helped Calvin to his feet. Calvin was still groggy and Mike had to half support him as he staggered over toward the shack and sat down heavily on a bench that was there by the door. For a long time Lorry just sat there, then he stretched out his right hand and looked steadily at the torn flesh. "That'll get well," he said. "The next time I meet Wayne Hardisty, we'll both have a gun."

Lorry spoke softly, almost as if to himself, but Mike Conaway heard him and he felt as if Lorry had slapped him out of a deep sleep. For there it was, laid out for him as simple and as perfect as if he had planned it himself. Here was the answer to how to get rid of Wayne Hardisty without any risk to himself. *Easy now,* Mike thought. *You've got it. Don't lose it.* "I didn't want any part of that, Lorry," Mike said. "Rudy can tell you I didn't."

Calvin looked up and the confidence was back in his eyes. "You didn't want any part of it but you didn't have guts enough to tell 'em you sold us those steers, did you, Mike?"

"What could I do?" Mike said. "Tex had that gun on me as much as he did on Rudy."

"Wayne had more than a gun on you, Mike," Lorry Calvin said.

"Let the sheriff handle it," Effinger said. "I've had a bellyful of Wayne Hardisty."

Mike felt a growing panic. There was a way to get rid of Wayne here. A way ready-made. Throwing Wayne in jail was no solution; for Brod, the minute he learned the facts, would go immediately to Wayne's rescue, and Brod Manwaring, sick or not, still had power. Brod would back Wayne up because Wayne had handled this exactly the way Brod himself would have handled it. Mike said, "You better leave the law out of it, Rudy."

"I pay taxes," Rudy Effinger said.

"Brod Manwaring pays more," Mike said.

"I paid out hard cash for those steers," Rudy Effinger said. "I ain't gonna lose that money."

"All right," Mike said. "Then I'll pay you for them. Write me out a bill of sale and we'll say I bought 'em from you.

Lorry Calvin looked up, his interest quickening. "Listen, Conaway—" Rudy started.

"Shut up, Rudy," Calvin said. "Let the man talk." He turned his expressionless eyes and his quizzical smile on Mike. "You were saying, Conaway?"

"That I'd pay you for the steers."

Calvin flexed the fingers of his right hand. "How much, Conaway?"

"Four hundred enough?" It was well over what the steers were worth.

Calvin grinned. "Enough for the steers," he said. "Not enough for what you got in mind."

"The only thing I've got in mind is avoiding more trouble," Conaway said. "Happens my wife's sister is engaged to Wayne Hardisty's brother. That makes this a family affair. It's worth four hundred dollars to me to keep it that way."

"You think that will take Wayne Hardisty off your back?"

"I wasn't talking about Wayne Hardisty,"

Mike said. "Your personal fight with him is your business." He tried to sound off-hand.

"All right," Lorry Calvin said. "It's my business. I don't want to take another beating like the one I just took. I think I'll leave the country."

"And have Hardisty tell it around he run you out?" Mike said. He felt the panic again.

"I got no pride," Lorry said. He looked straight at Mike, all that assurance in his eyes again. "But I have got a price, Mike."

Mike's mouth was chalk-dry. "How much?" he said hoarsely.

"I'll think it over and let you know," Calvin said.

Rudy Effinger's gaze kept shifting from Lorry to Mike and back again. He didn't like any part of this. He said suddenly, "Keep your money, Conaway. Just give me four beeves. I got a meat contract to fill. That's all I want. Four beeves."

"We weren't talking about beef, were we, Mike?" Calvin said.

Mike looked at Calvin and knew he was looking at a killer. *Why not let it run its course?* he thought. *Calvin will take care of Wayne without any urging from me. Why get myself mixed up in it?* He thought immediately of Tex telling Brod what had happened here today. A thing as small as that might start it. Brod might start asking questions, and when he did, he'd ask Wayne. . . . The perspiration was thick on Mike's face and he could feel it gluing his shirt to his body. He was so close to a solution. Why couldn't he come right out and say what had to be said?

He swallowed noisily and said, "All right, Rudy. I'll see you get four beeves. No hard feelings?"

"Not as long as I get my beef," Rudy said.

"You, Calvin?" Mike said.

Calvin laughed softly. "That's up to you, Mike. When you figure you need a hired hand, come see me."

Mike pulled himself into the saddle. His hands were shaking and his throat felt as if all the water in the world would never moisten it again. He sunk his spurs with unintentional savageness and his horse jumped into a full run.

There was anger in Rudy Effinger as he turned to face his partner. "I won't have no part of killing," he said flatly. "I'm gettin' my beef. That's all I want out of it."

Lorry squinted his eyes against the gathering darkness. "Like I've told you before, Rudy," Lorry said. "You'll always be a butcher." He looked at his wounded hand and started flexing the fingers again. He thrust his hand out suddenly for Rudy to see. His voice was quiet and he spoke without moving his lips. "I'm gonna kill Wayne Hardisty for that, Rudy," he said without passion.

"You're crazy," Effinger said. "What the devil good would that do? They find Hardisty with a bullet in the back of his head everybody will know who did it."

"It wouldn't be in the back of the head, Rudy," Lorry said. He sounded as if he were talking to himself, sitting there like a hungry man anticipating a promised meal. "I'd want Hardisty to see it coming. I wouldn't want him to have any doubt about where it was coming from. I'd like to have Tex Blanchard and Brod Manwaring watching it."

"You're crazy," Effinger said again. "You always have been."

Lorry laughed softly. "You don't think I'll do it, do you? You think I won't do it, Rudy?"

"Do it and be damned," Rudy Effinger said. "But don't tell me about it. I don't want to know anything about it, see? I don't know if you'll do it or won't do it and I don't give a damn. Just don't keep talking about it."

"I'll do it," Lorry said in that same monotone. "I'm gonna kill Wayne Hardisty." His face brightened suddenly and he looked at Rudy with all the guilelessness of a surprised boy. "But why do it for fun," he said, "when Mike Conaway's willing to pay me for it?"

Mike Conaway spent a nearly sleepless night, dozing, awakening, fitfully. He was nearly positive that Lorry Calvin intended to kill Wayne Hardisty, but being nearly positive wasn't enough. He had to be sure. For if Wayne Hardisty lived it would be Wayne and not Mike who drove a herd of Anvil cattle to Montana. Brod had made up his mind to that, and Ruth and Mercy would see that Brod's wishes were carried out. *I'm supposed to stay here and be the perfect son-in-law,* Mike thought bitterly. *I have to take care of the little girls and see that no harm comes to them.*

Listening now, Mike could hear Mercy stirring around in the kitchen. He turned in bed and looked at the grey square of window. It was two hours before sunup, he was sure, and that fact too, as small as it was, furthered the growing rebellion in Mike. The entire business of his marriage and the responsibilities of the ranch kept pressing in on him like a smothering blanket. He wanted to get away from here—had to get away from here—but he had no intention of leaving empty-handed.

He got up and then dressed and went downstairs. Mercy looked as freshly alive as if she had been up for hours. She was cooking bacon and eggs and now she put down the spatula and ran across the room and into Mike's arms. She kissed him and said, "Sleep well, darling?"

"Well enough," he said. He pushed her away and wondered briefly what she would do if some morning he stepped aside and let her run into the door when she made that morning charge at him.

She hurried to pour him a cup of coffee. "You be around today?" she asked.

"Some reason I shouldn't be?"

She laughed. "You're as grouchy as a bear with a sore paw," she said. She came over and rumpled his hair and he thought, *If you don't stop doing that I'll break your arm.* . . . "You said you were going on the roundup," she reminded him. "I wondered if you were leaving today."

He had intended to leave today, but now he wasn't sure. He hated to be away where he couldn't know every move Wayne made.

He said, "There's some things around here need tending."

"I'm glad," she said. She pulled out a chair and sat down, put both elbows on the table and cupped her chin in her hands. "What would you like for supper?" she asked.

He put his cup down in exasperation. "Good God," he said, "I haven't even had breakfast. How do I know what I want for supper?"

"Mikie," she chided, reaching out to touch the tip of his nose. "Don't be so cross."

"Sorry," he said. "Had something else on my mind." His nostrils flared. He turned to look toward the stove and saw smoke curling from the frying pan. He jumped up suddenly and snatched the pan from the stove. "Can't you cook eggs just once without burning them?" he demanded.

"I'll eat those, darling," she said.

He felt like hitting her with the pan. That damn self-sacrificing tone she always used. . . . He said, "Forget it."

He sat down and started eating his breakfast and she watched him closely. Finally she said, "Did Dad talk to you about getting Wayne to boss the trail herd?"

"He mentioned it," Mike said, and was

immediately angry. The old man had talked the whole thing out with Ruth and Mercy, just as Mike had suspected. So they knew about it and they were all in favour of it.

"It's wonderful," Mercy said, as if that settled everything. "Have you talked to Wayne about it?"

"When would I have talked to Wayne?" he said gruffly.

"Then let's have him out to supper," Mercy said eagerly. "We could talk it over and settle everything." The idea was growing, until a business meeting assumed the proportions of a party in Mercy's mind. "It would please Dad, Mike. It would be wonderful. It would be like old times, Wayne and Ruth and me together again. . . ."

"How about Clyde?" Mike asked.

"Why, of course Clyde," Mercy said. Actually she had momentarily forgotten Clyde. "Mike, don't you think it would be a wonderful idea?"

"I don't know," he said. "Why bother me with that?"

"It's important to get it settled, isn't it?" she asked.

He slammed his open hand against the table. "Look," he said, "am I supposed to do fifty things at once?"

"Of course not, Mike. Only I thought—"

"Well, don't think!"

He got up abruptly and snatched his hat from the rack by the door. He stalked outside into the pre-dawn darkness and immediately thought, *For God's sake, don't have trouble with her. Not now. . . .* He turned around and went back into the house, took Mercy in his arms and kissed her thoroughly.

"Mike," she whispered against his cheek. "Mike, I'm so glad it's going to be Wayne instead of you that makes that trail drive. I couldn't stand being away from you that long."

He kissed her again and went back outside and thought, *Wayne's not going to make this trail drive. And you're going to have to get used to being away from me, girl, because damned if I'm coming back.*

CHAPTER
12

WAYNE HARDISTY WAITED until shortly after sunup, then saddled a horse and rode down to the home place where Clyde was staying. He felt guilty running out on his partners this way, for this was the day they were to start moving cattle on to Beaver Creek, but he had to know if it was Clyde who had bailed Lorry Calvin and Rudy Effinger out of jail.

Patches of ground fog lay on the valley floor and along the river, and riding up the Lombardy-poplar-lined lane to the old home place Wayne remembered back to when he and Clyde had been kids together, going to school with Mercy and Ruth Manwaring.

He could remember his mother only vaguely, for he had been young when she died, but he remembered her as a driving woman who never seemed to be still. He had heard people say that June Hardisty had worked herself into her grave, and in a way he believed it, for the ranch had started falling apart soon after his mother's death.

He remembered the funeral and remembered his father, an easy-going, affable man with a hundred friends, a man who was always knee-deep in things to do. Chris Hardisty spent all his time sitting down figuring out which job to start first. He never started any of them.

When Wayne was fourteen, he himself had taken over most of the business of the Hardisty ranch and when he had needed advice, he had gone to Brod Manwaring for that advice. The enthusiasm of youth had led him to believe things that weren't so. He was a big cattleman, running a big ranch. . . . And somewhere, along about then, he knew he had fallen in love with Ruth Manwaring. There was no way to know exactly when; it was more an awakening. He remembered now how he had told her of his plans to build a cattle ranch as big as Anvil. "I'll start with Beaver Creek," he had told her. "I'll have a house up there where the creeks fork. . . ."

Beaver Creek. It seemed that everything had been built around that range. He realized now that his father had been using the growing friendship between Wayne and Brod as a key to Brod Manwaring's pocketbook. That was like Chris Hardisty. Wayne could see him now, with that half-apologetic smile on his face, saying perhaps, "It looks like you and me are gonna wind up being related, Brod. If you could loan me a few hundred on Beaver Creek to see me through. . . ."

No use damning a dead man, Wayne decided. It was over and done with. He still had no idea what his father had done with the money he had borrowed. It was of no importance. Wayne's dad had always been tangled up in some kind of scheme, and none of them ever paid off. The important thing was, Brod Manwaring had foreclosed on Beaver Creek, and when that had happened, Wayne Hardisty's dreams had been over. He had talked big and he couldn't back it up; he had promised a girl the world, and hadn't even been able to hang on to two sections of land.

Can't you see that, Ruth, he thought now. *Can't you see how I felt, after all the promises I made finding out my dad had been using my friendship with you and Mercy and your dad?*

So he had had a choice. He could stay here and scratch, and watch the ranch continue to go down hill, for he knew then that as long as his father was alive there was only one way to go, and that was backward. Clyde had been no help. Clyde hadn't cared. His other choice was to go to Brod Manwaring and take the job Brod had offered him—a hired hand, working for wages, with the rest of the crew looking at him knowingly, thinking, he's one of us today; tomorrow he'll be foreman; in time he'll own part of Anvil. That's the way to get ahead, all right. Shine up to the boss's daughters. . . .

That was the extent of his opportunity here, and his other choice had been to go to another place. When he made enough of a stake he could come back and offer to buy Beaver Creek from Brod, for now he knew he would never be satisfied until he made it on his own. *Where did the time go?* he wondered. *Five years. . . . Did I expect you to wait, Ruth?*

He dismounted out by the well-gnawed horse trough and stood there a moment, letting his horse drink, idly remembering how he had made horse-hair snakes in this trough, remembering every inch of this place. The horse thrust its nose deeply into the water and sipped noisily through its bit. A thin ribbon of smoke trailed from the kitchen stovepipe. Wayne led the horse across to the sagging front porch, tied it there and went around to the back door. "Breakfast ready?" he called.

There was a long silence and Wayne stood there embarrassed, and then Clyde's voice said, "Come on in."

He went inside, into the familiar room that looked little different than it had twenty years ago. Wayne looked at his brother, and then, knowing no other way, asked, "Did you know Lorry and Rudy are out of jail?"

Wayne saw Clyde pause and thought, *That surprise was honest. You didn't bail them out.*

Clyde said, "I thought they'd get thirty days at least."

"So did I," Wayne said. "They didn't."

"Who bailed them out?" Clyde said.

"I don't know," Wayne said. "I'll find out."

There was a long silence and Clyde said finally, "That's my job, Wayne."

Wayne managed a wry grin. "Not all of it," he said. "Lorry and me tangled last night. I busted him across the legs with a club. I got a feeling that as soon as he's up to walking he'll be looking for me. If Lorry had stayed in jail, it wouldn't have happened. I'd like to know who got him out."

"How did it happen?" Clyde asked.

"Tex missed four cows. He asked me to give him a hand looking for 'em. We run into Mike; Mike went along with us. We didn't find the cows, but we tracked 'em to Lorry's old horse camp and saw signs of where they had been butchered. Tex and me collected four of Art Keyes' steers Lorry and Rudy had there."

"If there's trouble any place, you'll find it, won't you, Wayne?" Clyde said.

"Not on purpose, Clyde."

"You're crazy if you get mixed up with Lorry," Clyde said. "He pulled a gun on you once. The next time he pulls a gun it'll be cocked."

"It better be," Wayne said.

Clyde got two cups and poured coffee. He sat down and stared intently at his cup. "Seen Ruth?" he asked finally.

"Couple of times," Wayne said. He tasted his coffee. "She says she hasn't seen much of you."

"Been busy," Clyde said.

"A man ought to be able to find time for his courtin'."

Clyde looked up and a grin touched the corners of his eyes. "That's one place where I'd say you'd be poor on advice, Wayne."

Wayne caught the momentary good humour in Clyde's eyes and was glad for it. He said, "Clyde, as far as those cows go, the deal you and me had is still on if you want it. You know that."

"I don't want it, Wayne," Clyde Hardisty said.

"Hell," Wayne said. "We both lost our heads."

"It was more than that, Wayne," Clyde said. "If you want to know the truth, it's just that I don't like the cow business. I never have and I never would."

Wayne looked up quickly, unable to believe his brother meant what he said. As far as Wayne was concerned, there was no other business beside the cattle business. He stared down at his coffee cup and pushing his finger against the handle, turned the cup around. "Anvil ain't exactly a cotton patch," he said carefully.

"That's right, Wayne," Clyde Hardisty said.

"It would be hard to separate Ruth and Anvil," Wayne said.

"You decided that a long time ago," Clyde said.

Wayne looked at his brother a long time. "We been friends with the Manwaring girls a long time," he said finally. "It was natural Ruth would be upset about any trouble between you and me."

"I saw her that night after she stopped by the cabin to see you," Clyde said.

"She didn't stop to see me," Wayne said.

"All right," Clyde said. "That night, anyway. I didn't know she was in town. I rode all the way out to Anvil and then rode back in. I was tired, I guess." He grinned. "It wasn't a very happy meeting."

Wayne felt a rush of old affection for his brother. "What the devil?" he said. "You expect it to go smooth all the time?"

Clyde looked at his brother, started to say something and checked himself. "I guess that's so," he said. "If you are going to town, I'll ride in with you. Friday, ain't it? Ruth will be in."

"Sure," Wayne said. "That's the thing to do."

He went outside and got his horse and while he waited for Clyde to saddle up he thought, *Why can't a man be honest with himself? You're wishing right now that Clyde and Ruth had never fallen in love in the first place.* But they had, and now they had a right to their happiness. *I wasted five years of your life for you, Ruth, he thought. I won't let Mike Conaway come between you and Clyde. . . .*

Friday was a day Ruth Manwaring liked. She awoke each Friday morning and found a certain feel of excitement in the air—a feel of many things to do and too little time to do them in. She wasn't a girl who liked sitting around waiting for things to happen, and because that was so her father's illness had been a terrific strain on her. Mercy had been little help, but perhaps that was just as well. Mercy was a person whose life was crammed with good intentions, but somehow she always managed to get her own way.

Breakfast was over now, the dishes washed and put away. Ruth had taken a tray in to her father and talked with him a moment about the affairs of Anvil, knowing that was what Brod wanted most to hear. Brod's decision to ask Wayne to handle Anvil's trail drive had seemed to take a great load off the old man's mind. Thinking of that, Ruth thought, *He wanted you for a son, Wayne. He wanted that more than anything in the world, and I couldn't give him the one thing he wanted.*

For a moment her thoughts were sombre as she remembered her last meeting with Clyde. It had been an ugly affair, and ugliness was the one thing Ruth had never wanted between herself and any man. Clyde had said a lot of things that would be hard for Ruth to forget: he had openly accused her of being in love with Wayne. And he was partially right, Ruth knew. She was in love with Wayne, but love was more than a stir of emotion and a deep-seated respect. Love also meant that two people had to accept each other for what they were, and Wayne had never done that. The thing he had said there at the cabin—"I never wanted you to wonder whether it was you or Anvil I wanted to marry."

She looked in the mirror, brushing her

hair, and now the strokes quickened into small, angry movements. What did you want me to do? she wondered. Give up my heritage and come crawling to you on hands and knees? I would have lived in a tent with you if it had been necessary, but I wouldn't do it just to please your ego. Do you think your kind of pride is the only kind of pride there is?

She felt a small hopelessness that nearly spoiled the anticipation of this weekly trip to town.

There were so many little things that had arisen between herself and Clyde. There were his almost childish actions—his heavy drinking on several occasions, and then the senseless gambling that had almost gotten him into serious trouble. *I want my husband to be a mature man,* she thought. *Clyde isn't, and perhaps it's because Wayne has never let him grow up. . . .*

She finished dressing, giving herself a final critical appraisal in the mirror, then went outside to where Tex Blanchard had a team harnessed to a spring wagon. "Anything I can bring you, Tex?" she asked.

"A million dollars," Tex said.

"And what would you do with it?" Ruth asked, letting Tex help her into the light wagon.

"Eat it, if it would do Brod any good," Tex said. "How is he this morning?"

Ruth felt a tiredness she couldn't put aside. "I don't know, Tex," she said. "I really don't know. I'll talk to the doctor again today and see what he thinks."

Tex stood there looking at her a moment, then turned and walked rapidly away. She found herself wishing suddenly that Tex were ten years younger. It wasn't that she didn't trust Mike to handle Anvil. She was sure Mike could. But there was such a thing as knowing the country—knowing the feel of it—knowing the tradition of a place. *The way Wayne knows it,* she thought, and was angry because she had thought of it.

The drive into town was pleasant. It had been beautifully warm for a week now and the entire country was green. Fording the river above town, she turned into the main town road and saw Rudy Effinger and Lorry Calvin riding toward her. It was the first she had known about them being out of jail and the sight of them startled her. Calvin gave her a broad smile and tipped his hat. Rudy Effinger stared moodily ahead between his horse's ears. Immediately her concern was for Clyde, for it had been Clyde who had put the two of them in jail. Why couldn't

Wayne have left that affair alone? she wondered. Why did he always have to be a big brother?

She drove on into town and found Clyde Hardisty waiting in front of the Emporium. He stepped out without a word and tied her horses and helped her down from the wagon.

For a moment she stood there close to him and she felt a rush of affection. There were so many old memories between them—so many things in common—so much on which to build affection. But was there enough on which to build a marriage? She squeezed his hand and said, "I'm glad you're here, Clyde. How are you?"

He looked at her earnestly. "I don't know, Ruth," he said. "How are you?"

She knew then that they were through with pretending. It wasn't fair to go on like this. She said, "Let's talk, Clyde."

"We'd better," he said. He reached out casually and took her arm, and several old friends, seeing them, spoke pleasantly and smiled knowingly. "The hotel dining-room's open," Clyde said. "We could go there."

How will we say it? she thought. *How will we admit that we're not in love with each other? We're good friends, but we're not in love.* She smiled and said, "All right, Clyde."

It was early, and except for a drummer who was eating because there was nothing else to do, the hotel dining-room was deserted. Clyde and Ruth took a table in the corner of the room and sat down, the self-consciousness welling between them. They ordered a meal that neither of them wanted and when the silence became embarrassing Clyde said, "How's Brod feeling?"

"About the same," Ruth said, and suddenly she was tired of pretence, tired of avoiding the truth. She looked up and said, "Well, Clyde?"

He started tracing patterns on the table-cloth with his finger tip. "About the other night," he said. "I ought to apologize, I guess. I said a lot of things that would have been better unsaid."

"I'm glad you said them, Clyde," Ruth said. "They were things you thought, weren't they?"

"That you're still in love with Wayne?" Clyde said. He shrugged. "All right. I thought it."

"And still do?"

"One thing I've admired most about you, Ruth," Clyde said, "you're always honest."

"And if I told you I'm not in love with Wayne?"

"I wouldn't believe you were being honest," he said. He leaned forward suddenly and put his hand over her hand, there on the table top. "Ruth, I'm not blaming you. It's just that—"

"It's just that you don't love me?"

"Ruth, I do love you. I've always loved you."

She turned his hand and squeezed his fingers. "I believe you, Clyde," she said. "You do love me. The same way Wayne and Mercy love each other. As friends."

"Ruth, I feel like a fool."

"Don't, Clyde."

"It isn't right."

"Because people will say I failed to hold my man again?"

"I won't let them say it," Clyde said. "I'll say it was the other way around."

The waitress brought the food and set it between them. Clyde looked at his plate, a long time and then looked up. "Are you hungry, Ruth?

"No," she said, "but if you had a bottle hidden some place I'd sneak out and have a drink with you."

They both started to laugh and he got up

suddenly and came and stood by her and when she looked up at him she saw that same wide, boyish grin that had first attracted her to him and she saw the old laughter in his eyes. "Don't eat that stuff," he said. "Let's wait until we're really hungry and than I'll buy you the biggest steak in this town."

She gave him her hand. "It's a deal," she said, "and I'll hold you to it."

She walked to the cashier with him. The cashier glanced toward the table they had just left and said, "What's the matter, Ruth? Was there something wrong with the food?"

"Nothing wrong with the food and nothing wrong with the company, Mary," Ruth Manwaring said. "We just wanted to see what it would be like to order a meal and not eat it."

When they had stepped outside Clyde said, "You know, Ruth, that was pretty good."

"What was?"

"What you just said." He took her hand and squeezed it firmly. "That's what happened to us, Ruth. We ordered a big meal but when it came to sitting down and eating it, we just weren't hungry enough."

"Go have that drink," she said. "There's no use both of us missing it."

184

She watched him saunter on down the street and she felt as if a great weight had been lifted from her. *You've really suffered through this, haven't you, Clyde?* she thought. She was momentarily sorry for him, and then she thought of herself and what people would be saying. Hear the latest about the love life of the Manwaring girls? Wonder who Ruth will get engaged to next, now that she's run out of Hardisty brothers? *Let them,* she thought, and immediately her thoughts were on Wayne. They were further apart than ever now, she knew, for now it was her own pride against his. *And I'm as stubborn as you are, Wayne,* she thought. *That's what's the matter with us. Why can't we be honest with each other, the way Clyde and I just were?*

CHAPTER
13

WAYNE HARDISTY LEFT Don Lien's office and turned up the street toward the harness shop where he had left his horse.

The bail information on Lorry Calvin and Rudy Effinger was a matter of public record, and Don Lien had handed it across to Wayne as such. For a moment the marshal had sat there, his tired eyes expressionless, and then he had said, "Part of my business is stopping trouble before it happens, Wayne. You better stay away from Lorry Calvin."

"Maybe you're worrying for nothing, Don," Wayne said.

"I'm not," Don said. He sighed deeply. "I've been marshal a long time. You get so you can pick 'em. You watch yourself with Calvin, Wayne."

"Thanks, Don," Wayne said. "I'll do it."

Don said, "And before you jump to any conclusions, remember that Mike Conaway is a married man with a lot of responsibilities on his hands."

"What's that got to do with it?" Wayne asked.

"A man like that tends to be careful," Don Lien said. "Maybe Mike would rather have Lorry Calvin for a friend than an enemy."

"I expect he would," Wayne said.

Thinking back on that conversation now, Wayne tried to find in it an excuse for Mike Conaway's actions. He might have been able to find it if it hadn't been for the incident of the four stolen beeves. Mike hadn't wanted to follow up those beeves; he hadn't wanted to press Lorry and

Effinger once they were found. That, to Wayne Hardisty, added up to one answer. Mike hadn't cared about those four beeves because he himself had sold them to Effinger and Calvin to pick up some money on the side. Mike Conaway, true to form, was finding it impossible to go straight.

The crime in itself was of no great importance. In all probability any one of a half-dozen small ranchers had done the same thing at one time or another. Brod Manwaring, because of his size and position, was considered fair game, and getting away with one or two Anvil beeves either for personal use or to sell to Rudy Effinger would be looked upon with a knowing wink by almost anyone except Brod Manwaring himself. But Mike Conaway wasn't a small neighbouring rancher. Mike Conaway was Brod Manwaring's son-in-law, and Mike Conaway was supposed to protect Brod's interests, not steal from him. . . .

The old pattern of Mike's behaviour was taking shape, and if it had gone this far, it would go further. Wayne knew the signs. He had seen Mike fired from a job in Wyoming for a stunt such as this; he had seen too many things. This was just one more link in a chain of behaviour that proved to

Wayne that Mike Conaway hadn't changed and never would change.

Wayne turned in at the harness shop and leaned against the greasy counter, enjoying the thick fragrance of leather. The harness-maker looked up and said, "You come in to buy that new saddle, Hardisty?"

"Not yet, Chick," Wayne said. "Mine's still holding together."

"I'd be ashamed to be seen riding that one," Chick said.

"Listen, Chick," Wayne said, "when I come riding down the street the girls look at me, not the saddle."

Chick laughed and said, "Say, that reminds me. You hear the one about the girl saw the calf with two heads?"

Wayne listened to a dirty story he had heard at least twenty times before. Listening to Chick's stories was part of doing business with him. When Chick had slapped his knees soundly and laughed himself out at his own joke, Wayne said, "What do you get for riggin' like that hangin' there by the door?"

Chick glanced at the severely plain black leather cartridge belt and holster hanging on a nail, then glanced at Wayne. He said, "Wayne, I wouldn't have no more trouble with Lorry Calvin if I was you."

"Who said I was?" Wayne said.

"I'll sell you the belt and holster for five dollars," Chick said, "but it won't make me sleep no better nights."

Wayne went over and took the new belt and holster from the nail and examined it briefly. He tossed it on the counter and said, "Wrap it up, Chick. I'll take it."

"Wrap it up?"

"Sure. I'm gonna give it to a young button for a birthday present. I whittled him out a wood gun that'll just fit it."

Chick folded the belt around the holster and got some old wrapping paper from under the counter. He wrapped the package and tied it with a string. "That would be a mighty good thing to do with it," he said.

Wayne took the package and started to leave. Chick said, "I'll take cash, Wayne. The last time I sold an outfit like that to a feller he didn't get back in to pay for it."

"You're a cheerful cuss," Wayne said.

"Then quit pushin' Lorry Calvin," Chick said. "That Calvin's a killer."

"It's funny," Wayne said. "He wasn't until word got around that he'd poked a gun in my belly." He paid for the holster and went outside. Keeping your business private in

189

this town was about like trying to store snowballs in hell.

He put the package in one of his saddlebags, along with the six-shooter that was already there, and he untied his horse and was starting to mount when he glanced across and saw Ruth Manwaring talking to Gwen Perkins there in front of the Emporium. He retied the horse and angled across the street. Gwen, a dark, pretty girl, looked up and saw Wayne coming and said quickly, "I have to run along, Ruth."

Wayne said, "I didn't mean to scare her away."

Ruth felt an uneasiness that was rare. She had just told Gwen about her broken engagement and that was uppermost in her mind. She had wanted to tell her best friend herself instead of letting Gwen hear it second-hand, as she surely would. Ruth flushed slightly. "Do you have to sneak up on people?"

"It's broad daylight, right in the middle of town," he said. He nodded toward the wagon. "How about a ride out to Anvil when you're ready to go?"

She thought of the long talk she and Mercy had had with Brod about hiring Wayne as trail boss and naturally assumed

Wayne's going to Anvil had something to do with that. "Sure," she said. "You can drive and I'll see the country."

"All right," he said. "I'll be around when you're ready. Anything I can help you with?"

"No," she said. "That's all right."

He turned and went back across the street and she stood there wondering if Wayne already knew about the broken engagement. And if he did know, what would he do about it? Would Wayne tell her he still loved her—that he wanted things to be the way they had once been? *And I'm supposed to cry with joy and fall into your arms,* she thought, and was immediately angry as she realized it would be hard to keep from doing exactly that.

She finished her shopping and found Wayne waiting. He tied his saddler to the tail gate of the wagon and climbed into the seat. Unwrapping the lines from the brake rod, he spoke to the team and drove through town, a hint of amusement in his eyes as he saw people glance toward himself and Ruth.

They talked of a dozen things—people they had seen in town, the weather, range conditions. . . . And by the time they were no more than a mile from town Ruth was sure Wayne knew nothing about her broken engagement. She knew Wayne well enough to know that he would have asked her directly, and he hadn't. She wanted to tell him herself, just as she had told her friend Gwen, but she found it difficult to do.

They forded the river and took the road to Anvil, Wayne's horse leading behind, and a hundred old memories stirred in Ruth as she remembered other rides along this road with Wayne sitting there so close to her and yet so completely far away. Once, there at the crest of the next hill, he had reined up and taken her in his arms without warning, as if he couldn't help himself. And for a few moments there had been nothing between them to keep them apart. He had kissed her, and it was a kiss she had remembered, and then he had said, "Some day, Ruth. Some day I'll have the right. . . ."

Wayne drove and Ruth sat half turned in the seat, watching his face. It was a face that was older than the last time she had studied it this intently. It was a face with an unyielding jaw line and a stubborn chin, a face that said, "This is Right. This is Wrong. There is nothing in between."

She wondered then what had actually made him decide to come along with her. He could have made better time going on alone. As always, she asked him directly.

"Just tired of riding a horse, maybe," he said.

"You're getting to be a master at evasive answers," she said. "Was it something about Clyde and me?"

He gave her a quick glance and she knew she had hit on the truth, but she still didn't know what degree of truth. He slapped the lines against the horses and said, "For two people who are about to get married, you two are acting pretty offish."

So that was it. She said, "Don't you imagine Clyde and I are old enough to handle our own affairs?

"If you see things straight, you are," he said.

"And you think we don't?"

"This business with Lorry Calvin and Rudy Effinger," he said. "It's gotten all out of shape and size."

"Who got it that way?"

"All right. Me," he said. "But it's past a squabble over a crooked poker game. Tex and me found out Calvin and Effinger stole four of your dad's cows. We took care of it."

"Oh," she said.

"Mike didn't tell you?"

"Why Mike?"

"He was with us," Wayne said. "I thought maybe he told you."

"I haven't seen Mike," she said. "He hasn't had a chance to tell me."

He wouldn't have told you anyway, Wayne thought. He said, "I wanted you to know the straight of it. People talk and get things mixed up."

Wait until they start talking about Clyde and me breaking our engagement, she thought. She said, "Still taking care of the world, aren't you, Wayne?"

"What's that mean?"

"If it was true Calvin and Effinger stole four of Dad's steers, I'm sure that Mike, with the help of the law, could have handled it," she said.

"Why pester the law?" Wayne said. "The proof was there.

"And so was Lorry Calvin," she said. "What are you trying to do, Wayne?" she said, angry now. "Find out if the rumours about him are true? Find out if he really is a gunman and a killer?"

"That's talk," he said, and knew it wasn't. "Anyway. that's got nothing to do with it. I just wanted you to know it was my affair and not Clyde's. If that's what you fought about, you both ought to forget it."

194

"Still taking care of little brother, Wayne?"

"Just trying to put you straight," he said. "I can't tell you two how to run your love affairs."

"Then don't act like somebody whose sister has been wronged when you find out that Clyde and I have broken up," she said.

"You won't break up," he said. "There's nothing between you two that can't be talked out."

"Maybe there isn't," she said. "If we wanted to try. We don't. I'm not going to marry Clyde. Now or ever. We decided that today."

He felt a quick stab of excitement and forced it down. "Why?" he asked.

"Because we don't love each other," she said. "Is that reason enough?"

He felt his hands tighten on the lines and when he looked down his knuckles were white. He said, "If it was anything I said or did—"

"Wayne, please," she said. "Can't you take it at face value and leave it at that? It's nothing anyone said or did. It's just the way it is, that's all."

"I'm sorry, Ruth."

"Don't be. I'm not a child." She was momentarily sorry for herself, wholly a woman. She said, "I'm used to finding out why men don't love me."

She was immediately ashamed of herself for saying that. It was a childish remark, completely uncalled for. She saw Wayne twist his hands against the lines and pull the team to a stop.

He turned toward her then and it was almost as if five years had never passed. He said, "If that's what it is, you better think about it, Ruth. You might be wrong about Clyde not loving you. You were wrong about me. I've never stopped loving you."

She wanted to be angry, and instead she felt she was going to cry and that was the last thing on earth she wanted to do. She wanted to laugh at him now, hurt him the way she herself had been hurt, and she couldn't do that either. There was no use pretending. She still loved him, as much as she ever had. She was there if he wanted to take her in his arms. . . .

He looked at her and felt the old longing, knowing that everything wasn't over, knowing it could be saved. He moved toward her and then checked himself, knowing he still didn't have the right.

He was going out to Anvil to have a talk

with Mike Conaway, Ruth Manwaring's brother-in-law. *Not yet,* he told himself. *Not yet. Talk to Mike Conaway first. Then see if she wants you or hates you.* He picked up the lines and drove on and, sitting beside him, Ruth Manwaring discovered that anger helped in holding back tears.

CHAPTER
14

WAYNE OPENED THE gate at Anvil and Ruth drove the team through, then closing the gate, Wayne climbed back to the seat and drove the short distance past the bunkhouse and up to the main house. There was a buggy there, the mare weight-tied. It wasn't a rig Wayne recognized and he wondered immediately if it was the doctor and if anything was wrong. Ruth said, "That's Phil Langley from Condon. He's Dad's lawyer." She let Wayne help her down then said, "Are you coming in?"

"Later," he said. "I want to see Tex a minute."

He helped unload the wagon, stacking the supplies there on the porch, then he drove the team across to the corral where Tex was waiting. The two of them started unhitching.

They worked in silence for some time and then Tex said, "Calvin and Effinger were out to see Mike this morning."

"Here?" Wayne said.

"Here," Tex said. "Pretty brassy, ain't it?"

"It's what I expect of Calvin," Wayne said. "A man like that likes to see how far he can push his luck, I expect."

Tex took his set of harness and hung it on a wooden peg in the barn. Without looking around he said, "Mike told 'em where to find those four steers you and me took away from 'em."

"Mike doesn't like trouble, maybe," Wayne said.

Tex turned and faced Wayne squarely. "You find out who bailed 'em out?"

"Yeah," Wayne said.

"You gonna tell me?"

"It's a matter of public record. Find out for yourself."

"I will," Tex said.

"You tell Brod anything?"

Tex shook his head. "You know Brod. He'd get all excited. He's too sick for that."

And too sick to hear that his son-in-law is stealing from him, Wayne thought. *Too sick to hear me say his son-in-law is a cheap, two-bit crook who has made a living by getting women to fall in love with him. . . .* He said, "Mike around?"

"He was over to the blacksmith shop a while ago."

Wayne turned the horses into the corral and then, without explanation, walked over toward the blacksmith shop. He found Mike riveting a halter and for a moment Wayne stood there in the doorway, unnoticed. Mike tested the repaired halter in his hands, then turned and saw Wayne. Wayne said, "I talked to Don Lien. I found out it was you bailed Lorry and Effinger out."

"You wouldn't have had to go to the marshal," Mike said. "You could have asked me."

"I suppose so," Wayne said. "You don't lie when you know somebody can prove it."

Mike had known he would have to answer for bailing Lorry and Rudy out. He had given it plenty of thought, tossing around in bed last night. He figured he had a convincing answer. He threw down the halter and said, "Why in the devil shouldn't I have bailed them out? What would leaving them in there thirty days accomplish? Just give them time to get madder, that's all. They would have gone after Clyde the minute they got out."

"And now they won't?" Wayne said.

"Now they won't," Mike said. "That was the deal."

"You're a liar, Mike," Wayne Hardisty said.

Mike's face flushed. "Listen, Hardisty," he said. "I don't know what you're riding me for—"

"I thought I made it clear, Mike," Wayne said quietly.

"What do you expect me to do?" Mike exploded. "Crawl on my hands and knees? So I was married once. I told my wife so."

"Twice," Wayne said. "If you call the second one a marriage."

"All right," Mike said. "She knows that too."

"The first time the girl's father gave you five hundred dollars for an annulment," Wayne said tonelessly. "It was all the money he had, but I guess he figured fourteen was a little young for his daughter to marry."

"You never made a mistake in your life, did you, Hardisty?" Mike said.

"How about Suellen? Was that a mistake too? Or did you marry her for fifty head of cattle and ten head of horses? It didn't take you long to sell out after Suellen was killed."

"How damn rotten can you get, Hardisty?"

"Not rotten enough to steal cows from my father-in-law," Wayne said.

Mike reached behind him and picked up the hammer he had been using to drive the rivets. All colour had drained from his face. There was only so far you could cover up and then you had to face it. He brought his arm around, the hammer held at his side. His lips were tight against his teeth. "All right, Hardisty," he said. "Just what do you intend to do about it?"

"I'm gonna beat hell out of you, Mike," Wayne Hardisty said. "I'm gonna beat hell out of you now."

He started moving forward and Mike raised the hammer.

"Keep away from me, Hardisty," Mike said. He took two steps backwards.

"You can only back so far, Mike," Wayne said. "There's a wall behind you.

Dimly Wayne heard Mercy calling Mike's name, then his own, and he realized Mercy was coming out toward the blacksmith shop. He hesitated, and Mercy was there in the doorway. "Oh, here you are," she said. "Dad wants to see both of you."

Wayne didn't turn toward her. He didn't want her to see his face. He stood there a moment, getting control of himself, then he said quietly, "Can it wait a minute?"

"It cannot," Mercy said. "You two haven't got anything so important to discuss you can't put it off." She came inside and took Wayne's arm, then reached out and motioned to Mike. Walking between them, her arms looped through theirs, she skipped a step to keep up with them. "My two favourite men," she said.

Ruth and Tex and the lawyer from Condon were all there in Brod's bedroom. Brod was propped up with pillows and he looked desperately tired. The lawyer said, "Do you want me to do the talking, Brod?"

"I can do my own talking," Brod said. He looked directly at Wayne, the old blustering anger in his eyes. He said, "You know the way to Montana?"

"Why—" Wayne asked. "You figure on running me out of Oregon?"

"I figure on getting you to take a herd of cows there for me if you ain't too stubborn to work for wages," Brod said testily.

Mercy was still holding Wayne's arm. She

squeezed it tightly. "You will, won't you, Wayne?"

"I don't get it, Brod," Wayne said.

"What is there to get?" Brod said. "Mike and me decided to sell some cattle. We need a trail boss. I'm offering you the job. You want it or not?"

"Oh Dad, you're not that tough," Ruth said. She looked at Wayne, and when Wayne saw her eyes he knew she was asking him to please say yes, telling him it was what Brod wanted. . . .

Wayne said, "It's a big job. I won't do it for free."

"You won't hold me up, either," Brod said. "Langley here has got the authorization papers drawn up so you'll be free to sell at the best price you can get. He's got a contract for your wages, too. Take it or leave it. I can get plenty men as good as you."

"Name one," Mercy said. She had snuggled her cheek against Wayne's arm.

"Don't spoil him, Mercy," Ruth said. "He's conceited enough as he is."

"Women," Brod grumbled. He looked at Wayne. "Well?"

"I told you a few days back I might have to go to work for you," Wayne grinned. "I meant it."

"Done, then," Brod said. "Now clear out of here, the lot of you." He seemed to notice Tex for the first time. "And you, Blanchard," he said, "don't get no ideas about going along. I don't want Wayne held up by some crippled-up old galoot."

"You ain't tellin' me what I'll do or won't do," Tex said. "I'm quittin'."

"See that you do," Brod said. "Damn good riddance."

There was no fire in the exchange. It was just a pretence between two men who knew each other completely. Wayne saw Tex turn and hurry out of the room, and Wayne followed. He had trouble catching up with Tex and when he finally did, Tex turned on him savagely and Wayne saw that the little man was crying. "He's dying, damn it!" Tex said. "Can't you see that, Wayne?" It was true, and Wayne knew it.

"I'll get on back to town and get the doctor," Wayne said. Mike was forgotten. That could wait. He untied his horse from the tail gate of the spring wagon. Tex had run down and opened the gate. Wayne spurred his horse into a run, somehow knowing that this was a useless ride.

As soon as Mike could gracefully get away

from Brod and the girls he hurried out and saddled a horse. Looking up, he saw Tex watching him and immediately felt the necessity of an explanation. "Going to town after the doctor," he said brusquely.

"Wayne already went after him," Tex said. "Better than a half-hour ago."

Damn Wayne, Mike thought. *Can't I make one move without him getting in the way?* He said, "Well, I got to pick up some things." It angered him to think he needed to give Tex an excuse, but there had to be some reason for his leaving the ranch. He mounted then and headed in the direction of town.

A mile beyond the horse pasture, sure that no one would see him, reined abruptly to the right and rode toward the hills. The darkness came swiftly, inky black except for the million stars and the irregular, white wash of the Milky Way. Mike found the Big Dipper and from that ascertained north, and he kept bearing that way across the high plateau that lay directly back of Anvil headquarters.

Coming finally to the bull-pine slopes, he found a ridge that seemed familiar. He turned left here and rode along it some way, worried now for fear he was lost, and then below him through the trees, he caught a wink of light and reined his horse that way. A few minutes later he made out the dim outline of the corral and the sagging cabin of Lorry Calvin's old horse-camp.

He reined in and with his hand alongside his mouth, called into the night, "Calvin! It's me. Conaway."

The light in the cabin went out and Mike waited, not sure of what he should do. After what seemed an eternity a voice nearby said, "Let's hear you talk, Mister." There was a double click as a gun hammer came back.

"Put that thing away," Mike said, angered at the start Calvin had given him. "It's me, all right. I want to talk to you."

"A man's got to make sure," Lorry Calvin said. "What was it you wanted to talk about?"

Mike was glad for the darkness. He said, "Did you get those four Art Keyes' steers back all right?"

"We got 'em," Calvin said. "You didn't ride all the way out here to ask me that."

Mike was having trouble with his breathing. It kept catching high in his chest. "What are you going to do about Wayne Hardisty?" he said bluntly.

"Maybe nothing," Calvin said. "Why?"

"You're crazy if you let him get away with

pushing you around like that," Mike said. "He'll never let up on you."

"Sounds like you know."

"All right, I know."

"Want him out of the way, Mike?" Calvin said softly.

"I wouldn't miss him," Mike said.

"It's a risky business," Calvin said. "The man that killed Wayne Hardisty would have to leave the country fast. It wouldn't be easy."

"You're supposed to be tough," Mike said.

Calvin laughed softly. "Why don't you do it, Mike?"

"Like you said," Mike said, "a man would have to leave the country fast. I can't do that. Not right now. I got a trail herd to make up."

"What's it worth to you, Mike?" Calvin asked softly.

"A thousand dollars."

"Two."

"All right, damn it! Two."

"Where you gonna get two thousand dollars, Mike?"

"I said I was making up a trail herd, didn't I?"

"That won't be your money. You have to ask your wife for five dollars."

"Not for long I won't," Mike said. "When I sell that herd in Montana or wherever, I won't ask anybody for nothing. You'll get your money. Do your job and leave the country. It won't be hard to keep an eye on a trail herd. You'll know where to find me."

"So you're gonna take the pay-off and just keep riding, is that it?"

"That's it," Mike said.

"How can I be sure I'll get paid?" Lorry asked.

"Would I tell you what I'm going to do if I didn't intend to pay you? I said I'd be easy to find."

"That's right, Mike," Lorry said. "You'll be easy to find." He laughed, a thin, wild sound there in the night. "Do you know what would happen to you if you tried to welch on me, Mike?"

"I know," Mike said.

"All right," Lorry Calvin said pleasantly. "We understand each other.

"When will you do it?" Mike said.

"Soon," Lorry said.

"He's in town now."

"Town's no good," Lorry said.

"Well," Mike said, "he won't stay there for ever."

CHAPTER
15

LORRY CALVIN WAITED until the sound of Mike Conaway's horse disappeared into the darkness, then he walked back to the cabin. "All right," he said through the open door. "You can come out from under the bed now."

Rudy Effinger started to curse. "What are you trying to do, you fool?" he said.

"Make an honest dollar," Calvin said. "Why?"

"You can't just go out and kill a man!" Rudy said.

"I have before," Lorry said. "Light the lamp."

He heard Rudy moving around, and then a match flared, the glow of it bright on Rudy's dark jaws, the light fanning up to accent the whites of his eyes. Lorry laughed softly. "You look like you're scared to death," he said.

"I won't have any part of it," Rudy said, putting the lamp chimney in place. The ill-kept room came into focus in the yellow lamplight and Rudy stood there, staring at

Calvin as if he had never seen the man before. "I won't have any part of murder, you hear me?"

"Yell louder," Lorry said, "and Wayne Hardisty will hear you."

"I got my beef back," Rudy said. He was breathing heavily. "That's all I want."

"You'll always be a butcher, won't you, Rudy?" Calvin said mildly. He was grinning broadly now, his eyes as hard as flint in the lamplight. He moved across the room, his movements smooth and liquid except for a small limp from the blow across the legs Wayne had given him. Reaching into a box nailed to the wall, he took down his gun belt and holstered six-shooter and strapped it on. Rudy moved back against the wall as if Calvin had slapped him.

"You goin' now?" Rudy said.

The masklike grin on Calvin's face widened slightly. "He's in town now," Calvin said. "That ain't the place for it. I'll wait."

Rudy came forward like an eager pup. "That makes sense, Lorry," he said. "You wait and think it over. All it could do is get us in trouble. You forget about it, Lorry."

Lorry shook his head. "I won't forget it, Rudy." He loosened the gun belt one notch and let his hand linger momentarily on the holster. "I'm gonna enjoy this, Rudy," he said. "I'm gonna enjoy it my way. My time, my place."

"Where, then?" The corners of Effinger's mouth started to twitch.

"Where Hardisty least expects it," Lorry said mildly. "Where else?"

"I tell you I won't have no part of it," Rudy said. "I got my beef. That ends it."

"For you, maybe," Calvin said. "I'm just started."

"You had an idea right from the first you could work Mike Conaway, didn't you?" Rudy said.

"I had an idea," Lorry said. "I was right. I knew from the first Mike was scared of Wayne Hardisty. I could smell it on him. I like dealing with a man that scares easily."

"Then leave it alone," Rudy pleaded. "We could have a good thing out of it. We could always get beef from Mike at our own price."

"If Mike was gonna be here we could," Lorry said. "But he's not gonna be here. He's gonna leave the country. Didn't you hear him say he was gonna leave the country?"

"Then let him leave," Rudy said. "We'll do all right without him. Why do his killing for him?"

"For money," Lorry Calvin said. He laughed softly. "You think two thousand is all he's gonna pay me?" Lorry drew his gun and spun it back into the holster. "He'll pay as long as he's got money, Rudy. While you're guttin' cows I'll be up to my hip pockets in money." His hand moved suddenly and effortlessly and the gun was out of the holster and even before Rudy had any idea of what was happening Lorry had struck the hammer with the heel of his left hand. Three shots rolled out so close together there was no way to separate them and there were three holes in the wall six inches from Rudy Effinger's head.

Rudy's knees sagged and his swarthy face went dead-white. He ran his tongue across his lips. "What the devil you trying to do?"

"Just limberin' up," Lorry said. "I haven't used this gun for quite a while."

"You'll have somebody over here asking what the shooting's about!"

"I doubt it," Lorry said. "If I do, I'll say I was shooting at a coyote. Any law against shooting at a coyote?"

"Listen, Lorry," Rudy pleaded. "When you came here you promised me you were through with guns."

"That was before I met Mike Conaway," Lorry Calvin said.

Rudy was quiet a long time. Finally he seemed to get up courage. He squared his shoulders and said, "I won't let you go through with it, Lorry. You've ruined things for me before. I'm not gonna let you ruin everything I got here."

Calvin holstered his gun with the same quick twist. It was a bit of showmanship, but it was done so effortlessly. . . . He stood there looking at Rudy Effinger and then he started to laugh, softly, deep in his throat. "You know, Rudy," he said, "I can only stand lookin' at you so long, then I get sick. It's always been that way."

"Leave me alone, Lorry," Rudy Effinger said. "You leave me alone, or so help me I'll—"

"What, Rudy?"

"Just leave me alone!"

"Scared, Rudy?"

"I'm not scared of you."

"Yes you are, Rudy. You've always been scared of me."

"Just stay away from me! Get out of here and stay out. I tried to give you a chance to go straight."

Lorry laughed outright. "You snivellin' little two-bit thief," he said. He reached out suddenly and clapped Rudy hard across the mouth. Rudy threw up his hand and Lorry slapped him again. "You wouldn't do anything, Rudy."

"Some day I will if you keep pushing me."

"Rudy," Lorry said, "you've been saying that ever since we were kids. You've never done nothing yet but talk, and you never will. You got a yellow streak a mile wide up that greasy back of yours. Go ahead and stay around and finally get yourself hung for a thirty-dollar cow. If I hang, I'll hang for something worth while."

"Lorry, be reasonable," Rudy pleaded. "Do you think I could stay here if you killed Hardisty? They'd run me out, Lorry."

"Or maybe hang you," Lorry said. "Maybe they'd think you did it." He stared at Rudy with that fixed grin, then shook his head. "No," he said. "They wouldn't. Nobody would figure you had that much guts." He went across suddenly and sat down on the edge of the bunk and started pulling off his boots. After a moment he took off his trousers and looked at the wicked bruise across his thighs. "It'll be a pleasure to kill Hardisty," he said, almost as if to himself. "A real pleasure." He glanced up quickly and grinned at Effinger. "It's the kind of job a man can take some pride in," he said.

"Too bad you can't sell tickets," Effinger said. "Too bad you can't arrange for everybody to see it." The mixture of fear and disgust was plain in his eyes. "Too bad you can't invite the Manwaring girls and Tex Blanchard, and maybe even the old man."

The humour in Lorry Calvin's eyes was genuine now. "You know, Rudy," he said, "I've been thinking that very thing."

Rudy sat down at the table and lowered his head on his folded arms. In a little while he began to shake as if he had a chill. Lorry Calvin, stretched out on the bunk, started to snore. Rudy watched him a long time, then he got up and went outside and saddled his horse. He led the animal a full half-mile from the house before he mounted, then he headed for town. He didn't have any idea what he was going to do. He just knew he didn't want any part of murder.

It was well after dark that night before the doctor finished with his house calls and headed out for Anvil. He questioned Wayne briefly and then shook his head. "Brod's lived three months past his time now," the doctor said. "I doubt there's much I can do."

"Will it happen fast?" Wayne asked.

The doctor spread his hands. "No way of knowing."

"I'll be out tomorrow," Wayne said. "Tell Ruth I'll get hold of Clyde. I'll talk to Gwen Perkins too. The girls ought to have somebody staying with them."

"That's a good idea, Wayne," the doctor said.

Wayne rode his horse up to the stable and turned it over to Pete's night man. The night man looked at the horse and said, "Who'd you run a race with?"

"Came in after the doctor," Wayne said. "Brod's pretty sick."

"The devil you say!"

"Got a horse I can use?"

"Sure."

"I'll go down and eat something first," Wayne said. "I haven't had supper yet."

"The Chinaman's still open," the night man said, glancing at his pocket watch.

Wayne walked back downtown. He went into the restaurant and ordered a steak and he had just started eating when a cowboy he knew stopped in for a cup of coffee. The rider grinned at Wayne and said, "Lee Leatherman's looking for you."

"With a shotgun?" Wayne asked.

The rider laughed. "Just about. He says if you don't start doing your share of the work he's gonna cut out your cows and drive 'em in the river."

"Wouldn't blame him much," Wayne said. He gave the rider an appraising glance and said, "You working, Jeff?"

Jeff grinned sheepishly. "I'm sorta between jobs, as the feller says."

"I can use you," Wayne said.

"I'm available," Jeff said.

"Go on out and give Leatherman and Newton and Faull a hand moving their stuff and mine over to Beaver Creek, will yuh?" Wayne said. "If you need anything, go on down to the Emporium and get it and charge it to me. Forty and found, and I'll settle with you when we turn the herd over to the Montana buyer."

"You hired yourself a boy," Jeff said.

Wayne cut a sizable piece of steak. "This is a fair hunk of cow," he said. "Why don't you have one, Jeff?"

Jeff scratched the back of his neck and wrinkled his brow. "Might do it," he said. "I hate to see a man eat alone."

"Hey, Too Damn Long," Wayne called to the Chinaman. "Cook up another one of these steaks, will you?"

217

"Too late," the Chinaman muttered. "No can do."

"Ah, go on," Wayne said. "You've only been here since four this morning."

"Too damn long!" The Chinaman said, tossing a steak in the pan.

Wayne nudged Jeff and both men laughed. "I knew he'd say it," Wayne said.

When the two men had finished eating they stood in front of the restaurant a moment, working with toothpicks. Wayne said, "You can stay up at my cabin, Jeff. That blaze-face sorrel is a middling good cutting horse. I'd use him. I'll see you in the morning."

"Thanks for the job, Wayne," Jeff said.

"I'm glad I run into you," Wayne said.

Wayne looked up the street towards the Perkins place but was unable to determine if there was a light on there. He walked the two blocks and saw a light in the kitchen. Going around the house, he knocked at the back door, saying immediately, "It's Wayne."

Bill Perkins, Gwen's father, came to the door. Bill was a thick, amiable, North Carolina man and he ran the town's furniture store and undertaking parlour. "Come in, Wayne," he said. "I was just fixin' to turn in."

"Gwen up?" Wayne asked.

"She was a while ago," Bill said. "Something wrong, Wayne?"

"Brod's taken a pretty bad turn," Wayne said. "I figured Gwen would want to go out and stay with Ruth and Mercy."

"Yeah, she would," Bill said. He took out his watch and looked at it. "Real bad, huh?"

"Doc seems to think this is the end of the road."

"Did you want to take Gwen out now? Was that it?"

"I doubt there's much use of it," Wayne said. "Doc's out there. He'll see the girls get some sleep. Clyde will be going out first thing in the morning."

"Well, I'll tell her," Bill said. He shook his head. "Seems too bad, don't it? Lucky Mercy got married, I guess. At least there's a man around the place."

"Yeah," Wayne said. "That's right."

He left then and went back up to the stable and picked up the horse the night man had for him. Looking at the animal, Wayne said, "You reckon this horse will last out the night?"

"That's a fine piece of horse flesh," the stableman said.

"Sure is," Wayne said. "Any crow would agree to that."

"Beats walkin', don't it?"

"Just," Wayne said.

The night was sharply cold and Wayne took his sheepskin-lined coat from behind the saddle and put it on. He had decided to spend the rest of the night at the home place rather than make the ride all the way up to the cabin and feed lot. He had to see Clyde anyway. Whatever trouble Clyde and Ruth had had was of no importance now. They'd both see that, Wayne figured.

He judged by the stars that it was well after ten o'clock when he got to the home place. He was chilled through and thoroughly tired, and the old drag of loneliness had never been more pronounced than it was at this moment. He unsaddled the horse and turned him out in the corral, then going around to Clyde's bedroom window, he picked up a handful of pebbles and started tossing them one by one against the pane. He heard Clyde's sleepy voice. "Someone out there?"

"Me, Clyde."

"Something wrong?" Clyde said quickly.

"Too blasted tired to ride on up to the cabin," Wayne said. "You got an extra bunk?"

"You know there is," Clyde said. "Come on in."

A match flared, and then the steady, yellow glow of a lamp filled the window. Wayne walked on around the house and entered through the kitchen. He paused a moment at the door of Clyde's bedroom.

Clyde sat up in bed. "You look like you've been drug through a knothole," Clyde said.

"I come in to get the doctor for Brod," Wayne said. "Brod's dying." And suddenly he wanted to talk—knew he had to talk. He came into the room and sat down heavily on the edge of Clyde's bed and for a moment he held his face in his hands. He looked up then and said bluntly, "Mike's been stealing cows from Brod, and selling them to Effinger and Calvin."

Clyde was immediately alert. "That's a rough thing to say about a man unless you're sure."

"I'm sure," Wayne said tiredly. "That's the trouble. I'm too damn sure."

Clyde said, "You've expected something like this, haven't you?"

"I was afraid of it," Wayne said.

There was a long silence and Clyde said, "You want to tell me the rest of it?"

For a long time Wayne sat there, staring

at the floor, and all he knew about Mike Conaway and all he suspected kept building in him until it had to have an outlet. He wondered then why he hadn't talked to Clyde before this, and thinking back to the trouble that had kept growing between himself and Clyde, he knew he couldn't have. There was nothing to go on anyway. It was one man's word against another, and Clyde would have taken Mike's word over Wayne's. But now suddenly it seemed all right to talk to Clyde and he knew why it was all right. Now, for the first time, there was something tangible against Mike, something that could be held up and seen. . . .

Wayne said, "It's a long story, Clyde. Mike and I started out as friends. We had a lot of good times. It started breaking up when Mike married a fourteen-year-old girl and made her father pay out five hundred dollars before Mike would consent to an annulment. I didn't see Mike for a while after that. He started living with a woman in Cheyenne. I heard he stole three hundred dollars from her and walked out on her. Maybe it was so, maybe it wasn't. I don't know."

Clyde wasn't interrupting. He was just sitting there, watching his brother's face. Finally he said, "He told me he had been married. Said his place was robbed and his wife killed. Was that so, Wayne?"

"She was killed, all right," Wayne said. "Mike wasn't married to her. That's neither here nor there now. I joined a posse along with Mike and we spent two weeks looking for the killer. Never found a trace."

"Mike take it pretty hard?"

"I thought so at the time," Wayne said. "He sold off what little stock there was and left the country. Said he had to get away from the memories."

"Then you came here and found out he had married Mercy.

"That's the size of it, Clyde." He stood up suddenly. "The hell of it is, I'm the one that's responsible for him even knowing about Mercy. I used to talk about Anvil a lot. I'd get to talking about Oregon and maybe I was homesick, I don't know, but I always wound up talking about Brod and Ruth and Mercy." He turned suddenly. "Damn it, don't it fit a pattern? If I hadn't talked about Ruth and Mercy so much, he never would have known about them, would he?"

"You're making a pretty big statement, Wayne," Clyde said quietly. "If you got to looking into the pasts of the most respectable men in this country you'd probably find they sowed a few wild oats along the way."

"You think I haven't thought about that?" Wayne said. "You think I haven't wanted Mike to have a chance?"

"I guess you have, Wayne," Clyde said. "You've kept still."

"What else could I do?"

"Nothing." There was a long silence and Clyde said, "What now, Wayne?"

"Nothing again," Wayne said. "I went out there today with my mind made up I was going to beat hell out of him. I didn't do it. What good would it have done anyway? You know Mercy. I never knew a time she wasn't taking care of a stray calf."

"You can't start anything now," Clyde said. "Not with the old man sick and the girls upset."

"So I keep doing nothing," Wayne said. "Mike hasn't broken any laws. He's got a legal right to sell Anvil cows."

"You better leave it alone, Wayne."

"Leave it alone," Wayne said. "He'll run Anvil into the ground and one day he'll walk out on Mercy."

"You don't know it."

"I know Mike Conaway."

"Suppose you're right? Suppose Mike does run out on Mercy?"

"I'll kill him," Wayne said. "He knows it."

"All right, then," Clyde said. "There's nothing more to do. You better get some sleep."

Clyde blew out the lamp and for a long time he lay there staring at the ceiling, thinking over what Wayne had said, knowing his brother at this moment better than he had ever known him in his life. *And I thought you were a man who rode trouble because you liked trouble,* he thought. He dozed off finally with the realization that it hadn't been only the avoidance of an additional five-mile ride that had brought Wayne here tonight. Wayne had needed to talk. *For the first time in his life,* Clyde thought, *he needed me. . . .*

As Clyde and Wayne made breakfast the next morning there was a new self-consciousness between them that made conversation almost impossible. Everything that could be said about Mike Conaway had been said last night, and both men were reluctant to bring it up again. They cleaned up the dishes and then went out and fed Clyde's horses. "I got to take that old crow-bait back to the stable," Wayne said.

"I didn't want to ride Baldy any further last night. I ran him all the way in from Anvil."

"Want to take one of mine?" Clyde suggested.

"No, that's all right."

"Baldy's a good horse," Clyde said.

"No better than that blood bay of yours."

"We ought to race those two sometime." Clyde grinned. "How about the Fourth of July?"

"I guess I won't be here," Wayne said.

Clyde looked up quickly. "What do you mean?"

"I promised Brod I'd boss his trail herd for him."

"The devil you did? I didn't know about it."

"I didn't know it myself until yesterday afternoon," Wayne said.

Clyde was thoughtful. "You like that kind of a job, Wayne?"

"Matter of fact, I do. Sort of scratches my itchy foot."

Clyde had his head against his horse's flank and was reaching under for the cinch. He didn't look around. "Leatherman and Newton and Faull figure you'll drift along, Wayne," he said. "Will you?"

"No," Wayne said. "Not as long as Mike Conaway's around."

"And when he isn't?"

"I don't know, Clyde."

Clyde looked at his brother and thought, *You're still too stubborn to tell her you want to marry her, aren't you?*

Arriving in town, Wayne was surprised to see Tex Blanchard. The old man looked as if he hadn't slept at all. He stood there squinting in the morning sun, his face drawn and haggard. He shook his head in answer to Wayne's question. "Brod's alive," Tex said, "but he don't know anybody or anything. Just lays there. Doc's gonna stay out there today, I guess. He sent me in to pick up some things."

"Gwen Perkins is going out," Wayne said. "You and Clyde can ride back with her."

"You be out later, Wayne?" Tex asked.

"This evening," Wayne said. "I got to go see how Leatherman and the boys are making out."

The three men stood there a moment more, talking, then Tex said, "Look who's in town."

Wayne turned and saw Rudy Effinger walking rapidly down the street toward them. While Rudy was still a half-block away he called, "Wayne, I want to see you."

Wayne looked at Tex and shrugged. "Guess he's gonna put us in jail, Tex."

"He is like hell," Tex said.

Rudy Effinger kept walking toward them and now Wayne could see the agitation in the man. There was fear written all over him. Effinger said, "I want you to see me right here in town. I want you to see what time it is, and I want you to see me here."

"What the devil are you talking about?" Wayne demanded.

"I'll have no part of it," Effinger said. The man was nearly hysterical. "I'll have no part of killing."

"Whose killing?" Wayne asked quietly.

"Yours," Rudy Effinger blurted. "Mike Conaway hired Lorry to kill you, Wayne. I heard him do it last night. Mike Conaway is gonna take an Anvil trail herd to Montana and sell it and run out with the money. Lorry's gonna meet him there and collect for killing you." Rudy was shaking like a leaf. "I ain't in on it," he said, nearly whimpering. "Would I stand here telling you this if I was in on it? I'm doing what's right, ain't I? Wayne, if Lorry finds out I told you he'll kill me. He's a killer, Wayne. He killed a man down in Texas for pay. Wayne, you listenin'? I'm tryin' to do what's right, Wayne. . . ."

Wayne had walked across to his horse and he was unbuckling a saddlebag. Every drop of colour had drained from Clyde's face. Clyde said, "Wayne, do you believe it?"

Wayne lifted the gun belt, holster and six-shooter from the saddlebag. He strapped the belt around his waist and dropped the gun into the holster. "I believe it," he said.

"Then don't be a fool!" Clyde said. "I'll go get Don Lien. We'll get hold of Sheriff Bud Stark. We'll toss Calvin and Mike both in jail!"

"On what charge?" Wayne asked. He swung into the saddle. "Go pick up Gwen and get on out to Anvil," he said.

"Hell with you!" Clyde said. "I'll stick with you."

"Your place is with Ruth, Clyde," Wayne said. He wheeled his horse before Clyde could answer.

"Bull-headed fool!" Clyde said. "What'll we do, Tex?"

"I'm gonna tell Mercy, for one thing," Tex said through clenched teeth. "After that maybe I'll kill Mike Conaway."

Effinger said, "I didn't have anything to

do with it, I tell you. If I had had anything to do with it would I be telling you?"

"Shut up, Effinger," Clyde Hardisty said. "Shut up before I knock your teeth down your throat."

"I'm gonna leave town," Effinger whimpered. "I'm gonna get the hell out of this country."

CHAPTER
16

IT WAS THE middle of the afternoon when Mike Conaway, coming across from the blacksmith shop, saw Tex Blanchard come out of the white house. Mike stopped and almost immediately sensed something wrong.

All morning he had been saddled with this impending feeling of doom, jumping at every strange sound. Now he saw Tex stop and look at him, and a blind man could have sensed the unmasked hatred in the old cowboy's face. Mike waited, fully expecting Tex to come across and meet him, but instead he saw a certain hopelessness cross Blanchard's face and then Tex went on across to the bunkhouse.

Mike walked slowly to the house, thinking. *The fool wouldn't have picked this time to tell Mercy I stole a few cows, surely.* He entered by the kitchen door and saw Mercy sitting there at the table, her hands gripped in front of her, staring into space. For a long moment Mike stood there, his heart thudding hard. This is no time for trouble with her, he kept thinking. Not yet. Not until Wayne is out of the way. . . . He forced a steadiness into his voice. "What is it, Mercy?" he said.

She looked around then and her eyes searched his face as if she were trying to read every thought that was in him or had ever been in him. She said finally, "Mike, why would Tex say such things against you?" She started to cry.

Whatever Tex had said, then, mattered little, for there was doubt in Mercy's mind about the truth of it. That was all Mike Conaway asked. He went to her and lifted her from the chair and held her close. "What things, Mercy?" he whispered against her cheek.

All the worry of her father's illness, the brutal bluntness with which Tex Blanchard had told her about Mike—these things piled together in hopeless confusion. "I can't even say it," she whispered. "I won't even repeat it."

"Then I'll say it," Mike said. He waited the proper time. "Tex told you I stole some beef, didn't he?" He didn't wait for an answer. "I sold some, yes," he said, "but I didn't steal it. There were some sudden expenses came up. I had to have some money. I just couldn't bother your dad with it and I didn't want to put any more burden on you and Ruth. . . ."

Mercy found her voice in a flood of words. "He said you planned to leave me—that you wanted to take that trail herd to Montana yourself—that you'd never be back—that you'd rob us. . . ." Her voice rose. "He said you'd hired Lorry Calvin to kill Wayne!"

Mike felt his fingers digging into Mercy's back. How in the devil could Tex have known that much? How could he have found out? Near panic seized him and he fought it down. *Think, Mike. Think fast.* "I never thought Tex would do a thing like that," he said quietly. He reached up and put his hand against her forehead and tilted her head back, making her look at him. "Mercy," he said, "I never wanted you or Ruth to know about Tex."

"What, Mike?"

232

Mike shook his head as if completely bewildered. "He's hated me since the minute I set foot on this place," Mike said. "He's made life hell for me, but I've kept still, knowing how Brod and you girls felt about him."

"Mike, why should he? He's got a job here for life, regardless of who runs Anvil."

"I've told him that," Mike said. "I've tried to reason with him." He sighed and pulled her head down to his chest. "Well," he said, "you might as well know the whole, dirty truth now. I wasn't going to say anything. . . ."

"You have to tell me, Mike."

"When I sold that stock to Rudy Effinger," Mike said, "Rudy spilled the beans." He paused as if he didn't want to go on. "Mercy, Tex has been stealing from Brod for years."

"Oh no, Mike!"

"Darling, I didn't want to tell you this," Mike said desperately. "I didn't ever want to tell you. I figured that what was done was done. . . ."

"Mike, why would he?"

"I don't know that, Mercy," Mike said. "I just don't know."

"But why would he say you hired Lorry

Calvin to kill Wayne? Why would he make a horrible accusation like that?"

"Can't you see, darling?" Mike said. "There's apt to be trouble between Wayne and Lorry. Everyone is talking about it. Tex was desperate. He didn't know I'd try to protect him. He thought I'd tell you and Ruth and you'd fire him. He'd do anything to discredit me with you. Even that."

"Oh, Mike, I didn't know what to think!"

He had won, and he knew it. He released her and walked over toward the window and stood there with his back to her, his hands clasped behind him. He said, "Mercy, I've never wanted to say this, either, but now it's got to be said. That night I came home and found my wife murdered. . . ."

"Please, Mike," she said. "Don't make yourself talk about it."

"I want to talk, Mercy," he said. "You've got to know. You've got to know how it was. When I left Wyoming I had made up my mind to kill myself."

"Mike, please—"

"I just kept riding. I didn't know where I was going. I didn't care. When I got to this part of the country I remembered Wayne talking about your father and I thought your father was the kind of man I might turn to.

I had to have someone, Mercy. . . ." He turned suddenly, superbly sure of himself now, a look of anguish in his eyes. "I came to see your father, Mercy," he said. "I found a new world and a new life. If you ever stopped believing in me, that world would be gone. I couldn't stand it a second time, Mercy."

She came to him then, into his arms, and Mike held her close. Looking across her shoulder he thought, *I'll have to stop Tex. I'll have to stop him before he talks to Ruth. Ruth isn't the fool this one is.*

He kissed her then and pushed her gently away and went into the living room. Going across to a roll-top desk, he took a small-calibre revolver from one of the drawers. He dropped the gun quickly into his jumper pocket, and taking his gloves from his hip pocket he thrust them in on top of the gun. He went directly outside and started toward the bunkhouse, then stopped flat-footed. Wayne Hardisty had just ridden up and was dismounting. Wayne Hardisty was wearing a gun.

The perspiration started on Mike's forehead. He couldn't face Tex and Wayne both, he knew that. Why hadn't Lorry taken care of his job? Mike's hands began to shake. He

235

went back into the house and sat down in a chair. In a little while Mercy came and stood behind him and started stroking his hair. "I believe in you, Mike darling," she whispered. "I'll always believe in you."

Wayne Hardisty paced back and forth across the bunkhouse and Tex Blanchard sat at the table, slowly tearing up a deck of cards one by one. "I should have gone to Ruth," Tex said. "I should never have tried to talk to Mercy."

"You shouldn't have gone to anyone," Wayne said hotly. "If I had thought it would do any good don't you think I would have talked to them a long time ago? What proof have you got? You think Mike can't lie his way out of it? He's spent all his life lying his way out of things. It's your word against his, and he's Mercy's husband."

"She called me a liar," Tex Blanchard said. "Little Mercy. I've taken care of her since the day she was born. She called me a liar." Tex got up suddenly. "I'll go tell Brod what kind of a son-in-law he's got! By God, Brod will believe me!"

"He wouldn't," Wayne said, "even if he could hear you."

"Then Ruth."

"You're telling nobody anything," Wayne Hardisty said. "You've done enough already." He walked across to the window and looked out. He could see across to the main house and Ruth was standing there on the porch. He sensed an aloneness in her that exactly matched his own feelings and he wanted to go to her and take her in his arms, not with any sense of giving her strength in a time of need but with a sense of sharing each other's strength, for he knew now that he needed her, too. He always had. He came back and sat down, then suddenly stood up and there was perspiration on his forehead. "Where is Calvin?" he demanded suddenly. "I've been out riding, giving him every chance to find me."

"Maybe he changed his mind," Tex said.

"Not Calvin," Wayne said. "He was up at Leatherman's place first thing this morning. He'd been gone about a half-hour when I got there.

"Wayne, why don't you let me get the sheriff?" Tex demanded.

"What then?" Wayne said. "What would it prove? Lorry Calvin could laugh in the sheriff's face and so could Mike. They could say we're imagining things."

"Get Effinger. Make him talk."

"Rudy's a coward," Wayne said. "That's why he talked in the first place. If he thought he would have to face Lorry he'd lie faster than a horse can trot."

"Then what are you gonna do?"

"What do you want me to do? Run?"

Tex's voice was desperate. "Wayne, why don't you face up to it? You're no match for Lorry Calvin with a gun. You never stood up to a man with a gun in your life."

"There's always a first time," Wayne said. He took his hat from the table and put it on.

Tex said, "Where you going?"

"To find Calvin," Wayne said. "I'm tired of waiting."

Wayne had ridden to the ridge above Lorry Calvin's horse camp when darkness overtook him. He led his horse into a juniper thicket and walked on a short way to where he could look directly down at the camp. He saw the four Art Keyes steers grazing there, but there was no other sign of life.

He was sure now that this waiting was a planned thing on Lorry Calvin's part. If Lorry Calvin was a professional gunman he would know the value of shattering a man's nerves. *Damned if I'll let him,* Wayne thought, then felt a grim humour as he realized fully just how tense he had let himself become. *Do something,* he told himself. *Get your mind off it.* . . .

But getting his mind off Lorry Calvin was about the same as a man with toothache getting his mind off the tooth. Lorry Calvin planned to kill him, and to Lorry it was just a job of work. Wayne thought of the assurance he had seen in Lorry so many times. *A man can be too sure,* he thought. He drew his gun then and held it in his hand. He was an excellent shot. He knew that. Real good, he thought wryly. *I've hit a running rabbit more than once.* The gun suddenly felt clumsy in his hand. Tex was right. If it came to a matter of gun speed, he wouldn't have a chance if Lorry Calvin was any good at all. . . .

He mounted wearily and started riding back toward Anvil, knowing no other way to go. The stars came out bright and sure, and night insects, sensing the nearness of warm weather, started tuning up in rehearsal for a long summer symphony. There was a lulling rhythm to the saddle and Wayne felt a sense of unrealness, as if he were a spectator watching this happen to someone else, someone he didn't know, and the sense of reality did not return until he thought of Ruth and Mercy and Mike Conaway. . . . He rode through a patch of scrub sage and the scent of it was pungent in the night.

He came finally to a place where he could see the lights of Anvil, and he reined up there, his hands folded on the saddle horn, and for a long time he looked down at the ranch, thinking of those lights as people. . . . One there would be in the white house and Mercy and Mike would be there, Mercy retreating from reality by refusing to believe anything evil. He had known it would be that way. There would never have been any sense talking against Mike to Mercy.

Beyond that was the light in Brod Manwaring's bedroom, and Brod was there, alive only in the sense that he was still breathing. And suppose he had told Brod? What right would he have had to ruin the few days Brod had left?

And Ruth? He saw the square of light that he knew would be the kitchen window. Maybe he could have talked to Ruth, but what good would it have done? He would merely have been asking Ruth to share a worry that was his own, for it had been no more than that until now. It would have accomplished nothing.

He could have told Tex or some of the older hands on Anvil, he thought, but again it would have been only the sharing of suspicion, the turning of those men against Mike. And suppose he had been wrong? Suppose Mike actually had intended to go straight? Would turning his own men against him have helped?

I did the only thing I could, he decided, and immediately he knew that this was the end of it. Tonight or tomorrow Ruth and Mercy would have to know the whole story; and if he, Wayne, weren't here to tell it, then Clyde would be. He had played the hand dealt him and he had played it in the only way he knew, but now Mike himself had asked for a showing of cards.

So it wasn't Lorry Calvin Wayne was facing, actually. Lorry Calvin was only a tool— only a gun in Mike Conaway's hand. He tried to find some anger against Calvin— some hatred that would make him want to kill the man. It wasn't there. If I kill you, Calvin, he thought, it will be no more than protecting myself in the same way I would protect myself against a rattlesnake. *It's Mike Conaway I'm facing, Mike Conaway and myself.*

The night was cold, but perspiration was

soaking through Wayne Hardisty's shirt as he rode on toward Anvil's gate. He dismounted and opened the gate, led his horse through and latched the gate behind him, then walked toward the bunkhouse, leading the horse. A square of light shone from the bunkhouse window and as Wayne walked into it a voice from the darkness said, "You were a long time coming, Hardisty."

The voice had a hint of laughter in it, like the voice of a man who smiles constantly. It was a voice that was confident and sure, the voice of a man who had a job to do and was getting pleasure out of the doing. Wayne moved away from the square of light, letting the bridle reins drop. "Sorry I'm late, Calvin," he said. "I was out looking for you."

Calvin's laugh was soft and velvety. "I figured you might be, Hardisty," he said. "Did it make you nervous, riding around looking for me?"

Wayne shifted his weight slightly, trying to catch sight of the man. "I didn't notice it," he said.

"Sorry you wasted your time," Calvin said. "Me, now, I like to do things the easy way. I figured if I waited around here you'd be along."

"You figure everything, don't you, Calvin?" Wayne said. He was still straining for a sight of Calvin and he felt as if the darkness were pulling his eyes out of their sockets.

"I figure everything," Calvin said. "Like I figured you'd be packing a gun. Did I figure that right, Hardisty?"

Wayne measured the distance to the corner of the bunkhouse, wondering if he could throw himself behind its protection. "Suppose you figured wrong, Calvin?" he asked. "Suppose I haven't got a gun?"

"Then you won't even have the pleasure of trying to shoot back, will you, Hardisty?" Calvin said.

There was a dim movement at the far corner of the bunkhouse. Wayne lifted his gun from its holster, the web of his thumb catching across the hammer, pulling it back. He heard a soft shuffle of sound and saw Calvin then for the first time. Calvin was standing there in a half-crouch and now the light glinted briefly on Calvin's gun.

In that second Wayne threw himself toward the bunkhouse wall and as he did, Calvin's gun roared. The blaze of flame seemed horribly close, the afterglow of it burning in Wayne's eyes. He fired at the winking point of light that lingered in his vision. He heard Calvin laugh, the most confident laugh he had ever heard in his life, and then he felt as if someone had clubbed him across the arm and he was driven against the wall. Only then did he hear the sound of Lorry's second shot.

In the house, Mike Conaway heard the first shot and jumped to his feet. Immediately Mercy had her arms around him, dragging him back. "No, Mike!" she pleaded. "Whatever it is, stay out of it!"

He shoved her roughly, knocking her down, and he ran outside, leaving the door open behind him. He saw Clyde coming at a full run, angling across toward him, and Tex was in the bunkhouse door, a shotgun in his hand. Two other Anvil hands were on the place and they came running in from the barn. Mike ducked as Wayne's horse broke and ran. There was a man there by the corner of the bunkhouse, but Mike couldn't make out whether it was Wayne or Lorry. Mike's breath was sobbing in his lungs. *The fool!* he thought. *Why did he have to come out here to do it?*

There was a sudden sound of running beyond the bunkhouse. Lorry Calvin, seeing the men closing in, was running for his horse. The figure at the corner of the bunk-

244

house moved away from the wall. It was Wayne. For just a second Wayne stood there, then Mike saw him raise his gun. He seemed steady—sure—more like a man at target practice. The gun exploded and there was a coughing sound out there in the darkness, the heavy sound of a man falling. Lorry Calvin's horse ran straight into the light of the bunkhouse door, the saddle empty. Wayne moved around into the light of the open door. The sleeve of his left arm was black and shiny in the light. Tex moved around the corner of the bunkhouse, calling to one of the others, "Here, with a lantern!"

In a moment Tex's voice said, "It's Calvin, all right. He's dead."

Mike stood there staring at Wayne. Wayne was slumped against the door frame, the light full on him. His face looked white and now the gun dropped from his right hand and he gripped his left shoulder and Mike could see Wayne's fingers squeezing the flesh. Tex was still out there beyond the bunkhouse. . . .

The full impact of it hit Mike Conaway then. Lorry Calvin was dead. . . . And if Tex knew Mike had hired Calvin, Wayne must know. Fear that was near panic gripped Mike. He saw Wayne turn and look toward him, saw the look in Wayne's eyes. Wayne pushed away from the door and started walking toward Mike. He seemed to reel a little, but he kept walking. Wayne said, "We've got something to settle, Mike."

Mike's hand dropped to his jumper pocket. He fumbled past the gloves and felt the small revolver. Some place behind him he heard Mercy call his name. The panic exploded. He jerked the gun from his pocket and fired blindly, directly at Wayne, and knew he had missed. He tried to squeeze off a second shot, and he heard Clyde shout, "Wayne! Look out!" and saw Wayne hit the dirt just as he fired again and missed.

There was a sudden roaring in Mike Conway's ears. He felt as if someone had hit him between the shoulders with a sledge hammer. He bowed his back, trying to escape the pressure, then he tried to walk forward, still holding the gun. He could no longer control his legs. His feet kept going ahead of him, jerking crazily. He fought against it and knew he was falling. . . .

There was a dead silence and then he was there on the ground, looking back toward the house, and Wayne Hardisty was standing there over him and the blood from Wayne's wounded arm was dripping down on him.

Mike kept staring toward the open door of the white house, staring at Mercy standing there, a smoking rifle in her hand. For a moment Mike saw her clearly, and then she threw down the rifle and was running toward him, almost as if through a haze. He could hear her sobbing, "Wayne, he tried to kill you!"

Mike Conaway wanted to laugh. It was Mercy who had shot him. The last person on earth. . . . He started breathing heavily, and now he saw Clyde and Ruth and Tex. They were all there, staring down at him, and Mercy was on her knees beside him, crying. *She killed me, and now she's crying,* Mike thought. . . . He said, "Wayne—"

"Yeah, Mike?" Wayne Hardisty said.

"Suellen," Mike said. "The half-breed girl." He fought for his breath and it seemed to him there was an hour's interval between his words. "I didn't mean to kill her, Wayne," he managed to say. "She came at me. I hit her. Knocked her down. I didn't mean to kill her—"

It seemed so important that he say that. He had to say it. He didn't want to die with people thinking he had deliberately murdered a woman. He looked up into Wayne's face, expecting to feel hatred, actually feeling a trace of old companionship. He said, "How did you find out about Suellen, Wayne?"

"You just now told me, Mike," Wayne said softly.

Mike Conaway started to laugh. He felt as if he were laughing, but he couldn't hear anything. "I never could figure you out, Wayne," he said finally.

Wayne turned away, feeling sick to his stomach, wanting to be alone. It was Ruth who came to him and put her arm around him to help support him. "I didn't know for sure, Ruth," he told her. "I knew Mike was no good, but what did I have to go on? Can't a man change? Brod was so sure. Brod had such a pride in being right. How could I go to him and tell him he was wrong on the most important decision of his life? How could I have told Brod, Ruth?"

"You'll never have to tell him, Wayne," she said softly. "Not now. Lets get the doctor for you. Dad doesn't need him any more."

Anvil's regular hands came in for Brod's funeral and they made their report directly to Tex and Wayne, knowing Wayne would discuss Anvil's business with Ruth and Mercy when the time was right for it. The crew had already been notified that it would be Wayne who would boss the trail herd that was being made up for the Montana drive, and now they were accepting Wayne's authority without question. No mention was made of the manner of Mike Conaway's death. Bill Perkins, the undertaker, kept Mike's funeral private. There was only the minister and Mercy present, and Mercy did not go out to the cemetery.

It was a week after Brod's funeral and the work of cutting out the two thousand head of Anvil cows for the drive was in full progress when Wayne asked Ruth to drive him over to where Leatherman, Faull and Newton were just finishing up moving their own pool herd on to Beaver Creek grass. Looking at Wayne's bandaged shoulder, Leatherman said, "Danged if you won't go further than any man I know to get out of work."

Wayne grinned. "We gonna come up with a thousand head all right?" he asked.

"Close enough," Leatherman said. He looked at Ruth uneasily. "Ruth," he said finally, "I don't know if this is the time or place, but we all been wonderin' if maybe we could sit down and talk to you about that lease we signed on Beaver Creek."

"You'll have to talk to the man who owns it," Ruth said.

"I guess I don't understand," Leatherman said, puzzled.

"Wayne owns Beaver Creek," Ruth said. "Dad left it to him. You'll have to talk to Wayne about the lease."

Faull and Newton had ridden up in time to hear that, and now Wayne saw his partners exchange glances. There was a twinkle in Wayne's eyes. "That lease looks all right to me," he drawled. "I always was in favour of signin' it but you boys kept talkin' against it."

"Danged if you aint gonna look funny with both arms in a sling," Leatherman said. There was a big grin growing on Newton's face and Wayne tried to remember how long it had been since he had seen the man smile.

"We might possibly work out something," Wayne said.

Faull shook his head and said, "I'm gettin' out of the cow business soon as I can. The wrong kind of people are startin' to own grass."

Later, driving back toward town, Wayne sensed the worry in Ruth and knew what it was. "How's Mercy now?" he asked finally.

There had been no way to reach Mercy since Mike's death.

"What should I do, Wayne?" Ruth said.

He shook his head. "I don't know, Ruth. Let time take care of it, I guess."

"She said this morning she'd like to take a trip. Maybe to San Francisco."

"Then I'd let her."

"I don't know, Wayne. She's never been away from home. Travelling by herself. . . ."

He thought about that for some time and then said, "Let's swing by and see Clyde a minute, shall we?"

They drove to the Hardisty home place and found Clyde saddled up, ready to leave. He had a bed-roll behind his saddle and when he saw Ruth he seemed embarrassed. Ruth looked toward the corral and it was empty. The entire place had a look of being abandoned. "Clyde," she said, "where are you going?"

"I couldn't say for sure, Ruth," Clyde Hardisty said.

Ruth looked quickly at Wayne, wondering if there had been trouble between these two again. She saw a strange wistfulness in Wayne's eyes and felt a small panic. She remembered when Wayne had left here, and she knew that Wayne, too, was remembering. She said, "You don't have to leave, Clyde. There'll always be a place for you on Anvil. I'd help you any way I can if you want to work up your own place."

"I know you would, Ruth," Clyde said. "Wayne offered me half of Beaver Creek."

"Then why leave?" she said.

"Ask Wayne," Clyde said. "He'd know."

But she didn't ask Wayne. There was no need of it. She knew now that there came a time when a man had to be his own man and make a decision of his own, even if it meant walking away from opportunity and security. Some men kept right on drifting. Some men found themselves. But a man had to know himself, and this was going to be Clyde Hardisty's way, just as it had been Wayne's way.

They left Clyde there and drove back toward town, driving a long way in silence and suddenly Ruth said, "It's partly my fault, Wayne, Mercy being the way she is. I always mothered her—treated her as if she were my child rather than my sister. When she married Mike, all I could see was Mercy's happiness. That overshadowed everything else. Even if you had told me how you felt about Mike, it wouldn't have mattered. I wouldn't have believed it because I never wanted to believe anything that would interfere with Mercy's happiness."

"It will be all right, Ruth," he said. "Clyde and Mercy will both be all right. Time takes care of a lot of things."

She looked straight ahead and thought of Wayne leaving for Montana with the trail herd within the next month or so. She said, "Has it for you, Wayne?"

He thought about it seriously. "I'll be back, Ruth," he said then. "Everything I want is here."

She said, "Beaver Creek?"

He reached over with his good hand and tugged on the lines, pulling the team to a stop. "No, Ruth," he said. "Not Beaver Creek." He put his arm around her and pulled her close to him. She lifted her face and he found her lips.

After a long time he moved away from her. "This danged arm," he muttered.

"Time will take care of that," she said. He looked at her and saw a hint of that old devilment he liked in her eyes. She said, "I'm glad you said what you did, Wayne. I wouldn't ever want to find myself wondering whether it was me or Beaver Creek that brought you back."

"That was a devil of a thing to say," he said gruffly.

"I'm glad you think so," she said.

They drove back to Anvil, into the gathering dusk. It was full dark when they arrived there and, pulling up in front of the bunkhouse, they saw Tex Blanchard, his saddle in one hand, his packed warbag in the other. Tex came stalking through the door and glared out at them. The full crew was back on the ranch now and the bunkhouse was a bedlam of noise. "I'm leavin'," Tex stated flatly.

"Good riddance," Wayne said. He nudged Ruth to silence and they drove on over toward the house.

As Ruth climbed down from the wagon she said, "What brought that on?"

"He sassed me," Wayne said, "I fired him."

"And just what gives you the idea you can go around firing my help?" she said.

"I don't know," Wayne Hardisty said. "It's just one of those ideas that came on me all of a sudden."

She laughed softly, knowing everything would be all right now. She moved close to him and he put his arm around her. It was dark there on the porch. It was an old, familiar darkness to Wayne and Ruth. It was a darkness they saw no reason to waste.